Satan's Diary
By Leonid Andreyev
Editing and Formatting by Anthony UylMTS

Devoted Publishing
Ingersoll, Ontario, Canada 2026

Satan's Diary
By Leonid Andreyev
Preface by Herman Bernstein
Editing and Formatting by Anthony Uyl_{MTS}

PREFACE

"Satan's Diary," Leonid Andreyev's last work, was completed by the great Russian a few days before he died in Finland, in September, 1919. But a few years ago the most popular and successful of Russian writers, Andreyev died almost penniless, a sad, tragic figure, disillusioned, broken-hearted over the tragedy of Russia.

A year ago Leonid Andreyev wrote me that he was eager to come to America, to study this country and familiarize Americans with the fate of his unfortunate countrymen. I arranged for his visit to this country and informed him of this by cable. But on the very day I sent my cable the sad news came from Finland announcing that Leonid Andreyev died of heart failure.

In "Satan's Diary" Andreyev summed up his boundless disillusionment in an absorbing satire on human life. Fearlessly and mercilessly he hurled the falsehoods and hypocrisies into the face of life. He portrayed Satan coming to this earth to amuse himself and play. Having assumed the form of an American multi-millionaire, Satan set out on a tour through Europe in quest of amusement and adventure. Before him passed various forms of spurious virtues, hypocrisies, the ruthless cruelty of man and the often deceptive innocence of woman. Within a short time Satan finds himself outwitted, deceived, relieved of his millions, mocked, humiliated, beaten by man in his own devilish devices.

The story of Andreyev's beginning as a writer is best told in his autobiography which he gave me in 1908.

***

"I was born," he said, "in Oryol, in 1871, and studied there at the gymnasium. I studied poorly; while in the seventh class I was for a whole year known as the worst student, and my mark for conduct was never higher than 4, sometimes 3. The most pleasant time I spent at school, which I recall to this day with pleasure, was recess time between lessons, and also the rare occasions when I was sent out from the classroom.... The sunbeams, the free sunbeams, which penetrated some cleft and which played with the dust in the hallway—all this was so mysterious, so interesting, so full of a peculiar, hidden meaning.

"When I studied at the gymnasium my father, an engineer, died. As a university student I was in dire need. During my first course in St. Petersburg I even starved—not so much out of real necessity as because of my youth, inexperience, and my inability to utilize the unnecessary parts of my costume. I am to this day ashamed to think that I went two days without food at a time when I had two or three pairs of trousers and two overcoats which I could have sold.

"It was then that I wrote my first story—about a starving student. I cried when I wrote it, and the editor, who returned my manuscript, laughed. That story of mine remained unpublished.... In 1894, in January, I made an unsuccessful attempt to kill myself by shooting. As a result of this unsuccessful attempt I was forced by the authorities into religious penitence, and I contracted heart trouble, though not of a serious nature, yet very annoying. During this time I made one or two unsuccessful attempts at writing; I devoted myself with greater pleasure and success to painting, which I loved from childhood on. I made portraits to order at 3 and 5 rubles a piece.

"In 1897 I received my diploma and became an assistant attorney, but I was at the very outset sidetracked. I was offered a position on _The Courier_, for which I was to report court proceedings. I did not succeed in getting any practice as a lawyer. I had only one case and lost it at every point.

"In 1898 I wrote my first story—for the Easter number—and since that time I have devoted myself exclusively to literature. Maxim Gorky helped me considerably in my literary work by his always practical advice and suggestions."

***

Andreyev's first steps in literature, his first short stories, attracted but little attention at the time of their appearance. It was only when Countess Tolstoy, the wife of Leo Tolstoy, in a letter to the _Novoye Vremya_, came out in "defense of artistic purity and moral power in contemporary literature," declaring that Russian society, instead of buying, reading and making famous the works of the Andreyevs, should "rise against such filth with indignation," that almost everybody who knew how to read in Russia turned to the little volume of the young writer.

In her attack upon Andreyev, Countess Tolstoy said as follows:

***

"The poor new writers, like Andreyev, succeeded only in concentrating their attention on the filthy point of human degradation and uttered a cry to the undeveloped, half-intelligent reading public, inviting them to see and to examine the decomposed corpse of human degradation and to close their eyes to God's wonderful, vast world, with the beauties of nature, with the majesty of art, with the lofty yearnings of the human soul, with the religious and moral struggles and the great ideals of goodness—even with the downfall, misfortunes and weaknesses of such people as Dostoyevsky depicted.... In describing all these every true artist should illumine clearly before humanity not the side of filth and vice, but should struggle against them by illumining the highest ideals of good, truth, and the triumph over evil, weakness, and the vices of mankind.... I should like to cry out loudly to the whole world in order to help those unfortunate people whose wings, given to each of them for high flights toward the understanding of the spiritual light, beauty, kindness, and God, are clipped by these Andreyevs."

This letter of Countess Tolstoy called forth a storm of protest in the Russian press, and, strange to say, the representatives of the fair sex were among the warmest defenders of the young author. Answering the attack, many women, in their letters to the press, pointed out that the author of "Anna Karenina" had been abused in almost the same manner for his "Kreutzer Sonata," and that Tolstoy himself had been accused of exerting just such an influence as the Countess attributed to Andreyev over the youth of Russia. Since the publication of Countess Tolstoy's condemnation, Andreyev has produced a series of masterpieces, such as "The Life of Father Vassily," a powerful psychological study; "Red Laughter," a war story, "written with the blood of Russia;" "The Life of Man," a striking morality presentation in five acts; "Anathema," his greatest drama; and "The Seven Who Were Hanged," in which the horrors of Russian life under the Tsar were delineated with such beautiful simplicity and power that Turgenev, or Tolstoy himself, would have signed his name to this masterpiece.

Thus the first accusations against Andreyev were disarmed by his artistic productions, permeated with sincere, profound love for all that is pure in life. Dostoyevsky and Maupassant depicted more subjects, such as that treated in "The Abyss," than Andreyev. But with them these stories are lost in the great mass of their other works, while in Andreyev, who at that time had as yet produced but a few short stories, works like "The Abyss" stood out in bold relief.

I recall my first meeting with Leonid Andreyev in 1908, two weeks after my visit to Count Leo Tolstoy at Yasnaya Polyana. At that time he had already become the most popular Russian writer, his popularity having overshadowed even that of Maxim Gorky.

As I drove from Terioki to Andreyev's house, along the dust-covered road, the stern and taciturn little Finnish driver suddenly broke the silence by saying to me in broken Russian:

"Andreyev is a good writer.... Although he is a Russian, he is a very good man. He is building a beautiful house here in Finland, and he gives employment to many of our people."

We were soon at the gate of Andreyev's beautiful villa—a fantastic structure, weird-looking, original in design, something like the conception of the architect in the "Life of Man."

"My son is out rowing with his wife in the Gulf of Finland," Andreyev's mother told me. "They will be back in half an hour."

As I waited I watched the seething activity everywhere on Andreyev's estate. In Yasnaya Polyana, the home of Count Tolstoy, everything seemed long established, fixed, well-regulated, serenely beautiful. Andreyev's estate was astir with vigorous life. Young, strong men were building the House of Man. More than thirty of them were working on the roof and in the yard, and a little distance away, in the meadows, young women and girls, bright-eyed and red faced, were haying. Youth, strength, vigor everywhere, and above all the ringing laughter of little children at play. I could see from the window the "Black Little River," which sparkled in the sun hundreds of feet below. The constant noise of the workmen's axes and hammers was so loud that I did not notice when Leonid Andreyev entered the room where I was waiting for him.

"Pardon my manner of dressing," he said, as we shook hands. "In the summer I lead a lazy life, and do not write a line. I am afraid I am forgetting even to sign my name."

I had seen numerous photographs of Leonid Andreyev, but he did not look like any of them. Instead of a pale-faced, sickly-looking young man, there stood before me a strong, handsome, well-built man, with wonderful eyes. He wore a grayish blouse, black, wide pantaloons up to his knees, and no shoes or stockings.

We soon spoke of Russian literature at the time, particularly of the drama.

"We have no real drama in Russia," said Andreyev. "Russia has not yet produced anything that could justly be called a great drama. Perhaps 'The Storm,' by Ostrovsky, is the only Russian play that may be classed as a drama. Tolstoy's plays cannot be placed in this category. Of the later writers, Anton Chekhov came nearest to giving real dramas to Russia, but, unfortunately, he was taken from us in the prime of his life."

"What do you consider your own 'Life of Man' and 'To the Stars'?" I asked.

"They are not dramas; they are merely presentations in so many acts," answered Andreyev, and, after some hesitation, added: "I have not written any dramas, but it is possible that I will write one." At this point Andreyev's wife came in, dressed in a Russian blouse. The conversation turned to America, and to the treatment accorded to Maxim Gorky in New York.

"When I was a child I loved America," remarked Andreyev. "Perhaps Cooper and Mayne Reid, my favorite authors in my childhood days, were responsible for this. I was always planning to run away to America. I am anxious even now to visit America, but I am afraid—I may get as bad a reception as my friend Gorky got."

He laughed as he glanced at his wife. After a brief pause, he said:

"The most remarkable thing about the Gorky incident is that while in his stories and articles about America Gorky wrote nothing but the very worst that could be said about that country he never told me anything but the very best about America. Some day he will probably describe his impressions of America as he related them to me."

It was a very warm day. The sun was burning mercilessly in the large room. Mme. Andreyev suggested that it would be more pleasant to go down to a shady place near the Black Little River.

On the way down the hill Andreyev inquired about Tolstoy's health and was eager to know his views on contemporary matters.

"If Tolstoy were young now he would have been with us," he said.

We stepped into a boat, Mme. Andreyev took up the oars and began to row. We resumed our conversation.

"The decadent movement in Russian literature," said Andreyev, "started to make itself felt about ten or fifteen years ago. At first it was looked upon as mere child's play, as a curiosity. Now it is regarded more seriously. Although I do not belong to that school, I do not consider it worthless. The fault with it is that it has but few talented people in its ranks, and these few direct the criticism of the decadent school. They are the writers and also the critics. And they praise whatever they write. Of the younger men, Alexander Blok is perhaps the most gifted. But in Russia our clothes change quickly nowadays, and it is hard to tell what the future will tell us—in our literature and our life.

"How do I picture to myself this future?" continued Andreyev, in answer to a question of mine. "I cannot know even the fate and future of my own child; how can I foretell the future of such a great country as Russia? But I believe that the Russian people have a great future before them—in life and in literature—for they are a great people, rich in talents, kind and freedom-loving. Savage as yet, it is true, very ignorant, but on the whole they do not differ so much from other European nations."

Suddenly the author of "Red Laughter" looked upon me intently, and asked: "How is it that the European and the American press has ceased to interest itself in our struggle for emancipation? Is it possible that the reaction in Russia appeals to them more than our people's yearnings for freedom, simply because the reaction happens to be stronger at the present time? In that event, they are probably sympathizing with the Shah of Persia! Russia to-day is a lunatic asylum. The people who are hanged are not the people who should be hanged. Everywhere else honest people are at large and only criminals are in prison. In Russia the honest people are in prison and the criminals are at large. The Russian Government is composed of a band of criminals, and Nicholas II is not the greatest of them. There are still greater ones. I do not hold that the Russian Government alone is guilty of these horrors. The European nations and the Americans are just as much to blame, for they look on in silence while the most despicable crimes are committed. The murderer usually has at least courage, while he who looks on silently when murder is committed is a contemptible weakling. England and France, who have become so friendly to our Government, are surely watching with compassion the poor Shah, who hangs the constitutional leaders. Perhaps I do not know international law. Perhaps I am not speaking as a practical man. One nation must not interfere with the internal affairs of another nation. But why do they interfere with our movement for freedom? France helped the Russian Government in its war against the people by giving money to Russia. Germany also helped—secretly. In well-regulated countries each individual must behave decently. When a man murders, robs, dishonors women he is thrown into prison. But when the Russian Government is murdering helpless men and women and children the other Governments look on indifferently. And yet they speak of God. If this had happened in the Middle Ages a crusade would have been started by civilized peoples who would have marched to Russia to free the women and the children from the claws of the Government."

Andreyev became silent. His wife kept rowing for some time slowly, without saying a word. We soon reached the shore and returned silently to the house. That was twelve years ago.

I met him several times after that. The last time I visited him in Petrograd during the July riots in 1917.

***

A literary friend thus describes the funeral of Leonid Andreyev, which gives a picture of the tragedy of Russia:

"In the morning a decision had to be reached as to the day of the funeral. It was necessary to see to the purchase and the delivery of the coffin from Viborg, and to undertake all those unavoidable, hard duties which are so painful to the family.

"It appeared that the Russian exiles living in our village had no permits from the Finnish Government to go to Viborg, nor the money for that expense. It further appeared that the family of Leonid Andreyev had left at their disposal only one hundred marks (about 6 dollars), which the doctor who had come from the station after Andreyev's death declined to take from the widow for his visit.

"This was all the family possessed. It was necessary to charge a Russian exile living in a neighboring village, who had a pass for Viborg, with the sad commission of finding among some wealthy people in Viborg who had known Andreyev the means required for the funeral.

"On the following day mass was read. Floral tributes and wreaths from Viborg, with black inscriptions made hastily in ink on white ribbons, began to arrive. They were all from private individuals. The local refugees brought garlands of autumn foliage, bouquets of late flowers. Their children laid their carefully woven, simple and touching little childish wreaths at the foot of the coffin. Leonid Andreyev's widow did not wish to inter the body in foreign soil and it was decided, temporarily, until burial in native ground, to leave his body in the little mortuary in the park on the estate of a local woman landowner.

"The day of the funeral was not widely known. The need for special permits to travel deprived many of the opportunity to attend. In this way it happened that only a very small group of people followed the body from the house to the mortuary. None of his close friends was there. They, like his brothers, sister, one of his sons, were in Russia. Neighbors, refugees, acquaintances of the last two years with whom his exile had accidentally thrown him into contact, people who had no connection with Russian literature,—almost all alien in spirit—such was the little group of Russians that followed the coffin of Leonid Andreyev to its temporary resting place.

"It was a tragic funeral, this funeral in exile, of a writer who is so dearly loved by the whole intellectual class of Russia; whom the younger generation of Russia acclaimed with such enthusiasm.

"Meanwhile he rests in a foreign land, waiting—waiting for Free Russia to demand back his ashes, and pay tribute to his genius."

Among his last notes, breathing deep anguish and despair, found on his desk, were the following lines:

"Revolution is just as unsatisfactory a means of settling disputes as is war. If it be impossible to vanquish a hostile idea except by smashing the skull in which it is contained; if it be impossible to appease a hostile heart except by piercing it with a bayonet, then, of course, fight...."

Leonid Andreyev died of a broken heart. But the spirit of his genius is deathless.

Herman Bernstein. *New York, September.*

Satan's Diary

January 18. On board the *Atlantic*.

This is exactly the tenth day since I have become human and am leading this earthly life.

My loneliness is very great. I am not in need of friends, but I must speak of Myself and I have no one to speak to. Thoughts alone are not sufficient, and they will not become quite clear, precise and exact until I express them in words. It is necessary to arrange them in a row, like soldiers or telephone poles, to lay them out like a railway track, to throw across bridges and viaducts, to construct barrows and enclosures, to indicate stations in certain places—and only then will everything become clear. This laborious engineering work, I think, they call logic and consistency, and is essential to those who desire to be wise. It is not essential to all others. They may wander about as they please.

The work is slow, difficult and repulsive for one who is accustomed to—I do not know what to call it—to embracing all in one breath and expressing all in a single breath. It is not in vain that men respect their thinkers so much, and it is not in vain that these unfortunate thinkers, if they are honest and conscientious in this process of construction, as ordinary engineers, end in insane asylums. I am but a few days on this earth and more than once have the yellow walls of the insane asylum and its luring open door flashed before my eyes.

Yes, it is extremely difficult and irritates one's "nerves." I have just now wasted so much of the ship's fine stationery to express a little ordinary thought on the inadequacy of man's words and logic. What will it be necessary to waste to give expression to the great and the unusual? I want to warn you, my earthly reader, at the very outset, not to gape in astonishment. The *extraordinary cannot be expressed* in the language of your grumbling. If you do not believe me, go to the nearest insane asylum and listen to the inmates: they have all realized *Something* and wanted to give expression to it. And now you can hear the roar and rumble of these wrecked engines, their wheels revolving and hissing in the air, and you can see with what difficulty they manage to hold intact the rapidly dissolving features of their astonished faces!

I see you are all ready to ply me with questions, now that you learned that I am Satan in human form: it is so fascinating! Whence did I come? What are the ways of Hell? Is there immortality there, and, also, what is the price of coal at the stock exchange of Hell? Unfortunately, my dear reader, despite my desire to the contrary, if I had such a desire, I am powerless to satisfy your very proper curiosity. I could have composed for your benefit one of those funny little stories about horny and hairy devils, which appeal so much to your meagre imagination, but you have had enough of them already and I do not want to lie so rudely and ungracefully. I will lie to you elsewhere, when you least expect it, and that will be far more interesting for both of us.

And the truth—how am I to tell it when even my Name cannot be expressed in your tongue? You have called me Satan and I accept the name, just as I would have accepted any other: Be it so—I am Satan. But my real name sounds quite different, quite different! It has an extraordinary sound and try as I may I cannot force it into your narrow ear without tearing it open together with your brain: Be it so—I am Satan. And nothing more.

And you yourself are to blame for this, my friend: why is there so little understanding in your reason? Your reason is like a beggar's sack, containing only crusts of stale bread, while it is necessary to have something more than bread. You have but two conceptions of existence: life and death. How, then, can I reveal to you the *third*? All your existence is an absurdity only because you do not have this *third conception*. And where can I get it for you? To-day I am human, even as you. In my skull is your brain. In my mouth are your cubic words, jostling one another about with their sharp corners, and I cannot tell you of the Extraordinary.

If I were to tell you that there are no devils I would lie. But if I say that such creatures do exist I also deceive you. You see how difficult it is, how absurd, my friend!

I can also tell you but little that you would understand of how I assumed the human form, with which I began my earthly life ten days ago. First of all, forget about your favorite, hairy, horny, winged devils, who breathe fire, transform fragments of earthenware into gold and change old men into fascinating youths, and having done all this and prattled much nonsense, they disappear suddenly through a wall. Remember: when *we*, want to visit your earth *we* must always become human. Why this is so you will learn after your death. Meanwhile remember: I am a human being now like yourself. There is not the foul smell of a goat about me but the fragrance of perfume, and you need not fear to shake My hand lest I may scratch you with my nails: I manicure them just as you do.

But how did it all happen? Very simply. When I first conceived the desire to visit this earth I selected as the most satisfactory lodging a 38-year-old American billionaire, Mr. Henry Wondergood. I killed him at night,—of course, not in the presence of witnesses. But you cannot bring me to court despite this confession, because the American is ALIVE, and we both greet you with one respectful bow: I and Wondergood. He simply rented his empty place to me. You understand? And not all of it either, the devil take him! And, to my great regret I can *return* only through the same door which leads you too to liberty: through death.

This is the most important thing. You may understand something of what I may have to say later on, although to speak to you of such matters in your language is like trying to conceal a mountain in a vest pocket or to empty Niagara with a thimble. Imagine, for example, that you, my dear King of Nature, should want to come closer to the ants, and that by some miracle you became a real little ant,—then you may have some conception of that gulf which separates Me now from what I was. No, still more! Imagine that you were a sound and have become a mere symbol—a musical mark on paper…. No, still worse!—No comparisons can make clear to you that terrible gulf whose bottom even I do not see as yet. Or, perhaps, there is no bottom there at all.

Think of it: for two days, after leaving New York, I suffered from seasickness! This sounds queer to you, who are accustomed to wallow in your own dirt? Well, I—I have also wallowed in it but it was not queer at all. I only smiled once in thinking that *it* was not I, but Wondergood, and said:

"Roll on, Wondergood, roll on!"

There is another question to which you probably want an answer: Why did I come to this earth and accept such an unprofitable exchange: to be transformed from Satan, "the mighty, immortal chieftain and ruler" into you? I am tired of seeking words that cannot be found. I will answer you in English, French, Italian or German—languages we both understand well. I have grown lonesome in Hell and I have come upon the earth to lie and play.

You know what ennui is. And as for falsehood, you know it well too. And as for *play*—you can judge it to a certain extent by your own theaters and celebrated actors. Perhaps you yourself are playing a little rôle in Parliament, at home, or in your church. If you are, you may understand something of the *satisfaction* of play. And, if in addition, you are familiar with the multiplication table, then multiply the delight and joy of play into any considerable figure and you will get an idea of My enjoyment, of My play. No, imagine that you are an ocean wave, which plays eternally and lives only in play—take this wave, for example, which I see outside the porthole now and which wants to lift our "Atlantic"…but, here I am again seeking words and comparisons!

I simply want to play. At present I am still an unknown actor, a modest débutante, but I hope to become no less a celebrity than your own Garrick or Aldrich, after I have played what I please. I am proud, selfish and even, if you please, vain and boastful. You know what vanity is, when you crave the praise and plaudits even of a fool? Then I entertain the brazen idea that I am a genius. Satan is known for his brazenness. And so, imagine, that I have grown weary of Hell where all these hairy and horny rogues play and lie no worse than I do, and that I am no longer satisfied with the laurels of Hell, in which I but perceive no small measure of base flattery and downright stupidity. But I have heard of you, my earthly friend; I have heard that you are wise, tolerably honest, properly incredulous, responsive to the problems of eternal art and that you yourself play and lie so badly that you might appreciate the playing of others: not in vain have you so many *great actors*. And so I have come. You understand?

My stage is the earth and the nearest scene for which I am now bound is Rome, the Eternal City, as it is called here, in your profound conception of eternity and other simple matters. I have not yet selected my company (would you not like to join it?). But I believe that *Fate* and *Chance*, to whom I am now subservient, like all your earthly things, will realize my unselfish motives and will send me worthy partners. Old Europe is so rich in talents! I believe that I shall find a keen and appreciative audience in Europe, too. I confess that I first thought of going to the East, which some of my compatriots made their scene of activity some time ago with no small measure of success, but the East is too credulous and is inclined too much to poison and the ballet. Its gods are ludicrous. The East still reeks too much of hairy animals. Its lights and shadows are barbarously crude and too bright to make it worth while for a refined artist as I am to go into that crowded, foul circus tent. Ah, my friend, I am so vain that I even begin this Diary not without the secret intention of impressing you with my modesty in the rôle of *seeker* of words and comparisons. I hope you will not take advantage of my frankness and cease believing me.

Are there any other questions? Of the play itself I have no clear idea yet. It will be composed by the same impresario who will assemble the actors—*Fate*. My modest rôle, as a beginning, will be that of a man who so loves his fellow beings that he is willing to give them everything, his soul and his money. Of course, you have not forgotten that I am a billionaire? I have three billion dollars. Sufficient—is it not?—for one spectacular performance. One more detail before I conclude this page.

I have with me, sharing my fate, a certain Irwin Toppi, my secretary,—a most worthy person in his black frock coat and silk top hat, his long nose resembling an unripened pear and his smoothly shaven, pastor-like face. I would not be surprised to find a prayer book in his pocket. My Toppi came upon this earth from *there*, i.e. from Hell and by the same means as mine: he, too, assumed the human form and, it seems, quite successfully—the rogue is entirely immune from seasickness. However to be seasick one must have some brains and my Toppi is unusually stupid—even for this earth. Besides, he is impolite and ventures to offer advice. I am rather sorry that out of our entire wealth of material I did not select some one better, but I was impressed by his honesty and partial familiarity with the earth: it seemed more pleasant to enter upon this little jaunt with an experienced comrade. Quite a long time ago he once before assumed the human form and was so taken by religious sentiments that—think of it!—he entered a Franciscan monastery, lived there to a ripe old age and died peacefully under the name of Brother Vincent. His ashes became the object of veneration for believers—not a bad career for a fool of a devil. No sooner did he enter upon this trip with Me than he began to sniff about for incense—an incurable habit! You will probably like him.

And now enough. Get thee hence, my friend. I wish to be alone. Your shallow reflection upon this wall wears upon me. I wish to be alone or only with this Wondergood who has leased his abode to Me and seems to have gotten the best of Me somehow or other. The sea is calm. I am no longer nauseated but I am afraid of something. I am afraid! I fear this darkness which they call night and descends upon the ocean: here, in the cabin there is still some light, but there, on deck, there is terrible darkness, and My eyes are quite helpless. These silly reflectors—they are worthless. They are able to reflect things by day but in the darkness they lose even this miserable power. Of course I shall get used to the darkness. I have already grown used to many things. But just now I am ill at ease and it is horrible to think that the mere turn of a key obsesses me with this blind ever present darkness. Whence does it come?

And how brave men are with their dim reflectors: they see nothing and simply say: it is dark here, we must make a light! Then they themselves put it out and go to sleep. I regard these braves with a kind of cold wonder and I am seized with admiration. Or must one possess a great mind to appreciate horror, like Mine? You are not such a coward, Wondergood. You always bore the reputation of being a hardened man and a man of experience!

There is one moment in the process of my assumption of the human form that I cannot recollect without horror. That was when for the first time I heard the beating of My heart. This regular, loud, metronome-like sound, which speaks as much of death as of life, filled me with the hitherto inexperienced sensation of horror. Men are always quarrelling about accounts, but how can they carry in their breasts *this* counting machine, registering with the speed of a magician the fleeting seconds of life?

At first I wanted to shout and to run back *below*, before I could grow accustomed to life, but here I looked at Toppi: this new-born fool was calmly brushing his top hat with the sleeve of his frock coat. I broke out into laughter and cried:

"Toppi, the brush!"

We both brushed ourselves while the counting machine in my breast was computing the seconds and, it seemed to me, adding on a few for good measure. Finally, hearing its brazen beating, I thought I might not have time enough to finish my toillette. I have been in a great hurry for some time. Just what it was I would not be able to complete I did not know, but for two days I was in a mad rush to eat and drink and even sleep: the counting machine was beating away while I lay in slumber!

But I never rush now. I know that I will manage to get through and my moments seem inexhaustible. But the little machine keeps on beating just the same, like a drunken soldier at a drum. And how about the very moments it is using up now. Are they to be counted as equal to the great ones? Then I say it is all a fraud and I protest as a honest citizen of the United States and as a merchant.

I do not feel well. Yet I would not repulse even a friend at this moment. Ah! In all the universe I am alone!

February 7, 1914. Rome, Hotel "Internationale."
I am driven mad whenever I am compelled to seize the club of a policeman to bring order in my brain: facts, to the right! thoughts, to the left! moods, to the rear—clear the road for His Highness, Conscience, which barely moves about upon its stilts. I am compelled to do this: otherwise there would be a riot, an abrecadebra, chaos. And so I call you to order, gentleman—facts and lady-thoughts. I begin.

Night. Darkness. The air is balmy. There is a pleasant fragrance. Toppi is enchanted. We are in Italy. Our speeding train is approaching Rome. We are enjoying our soft couches when, suddenly, crash! Everything flies to the devil: the train has gone out of its mind. It is wrecked. I confess without shame that I am not very brave, that I was seized with terror and seemed to have lost consciousness. The lights were extinguished and with much labor I crawled out of the corner into which I had been hurled. I seemed to have forgotten the exit. There were only walls and corners. I felt something stinging and beating at Me, and all about nothing but darkness. Suddenly I felt a body beneath my feet. I stepped right upon the face. Only afterwards did I discover that the body was that of George, my lackey, killed outright. I shouted and my obliging Toppi came to my aid: he seized me by the arm and led me to an open window, as both exits had been barricaded by fragments of the car and baggage. I leaped out, but Toppi lingered behind. My knees were trembling. I was groaning but still he failed to appear. I shouted. Suddenly he reappeared at the window and shouted back:

"What are you crying about? I am looking for our hats and your portfolio."

A few moments later he returned and handed me my hat. He himself had his silk top hat on and carried the portfolio. I shook with laughter and said:

"Young man, you have forgotten the umbrella!"

But the old buffoon has no sense of humor. He replied seriously:

"I do not carry an umbrella. And do you know, our George is dead and so is the chef."

So, this fallen carcass which has no feelings and upon whose face one steps with impunity is our George! I was again seized with terror and suddenly my ears were pierced with groans, wild shrieks, whistlings and cries! All the sounds wherewith these braves wail when they are crushed. At first I was deafened. I heard nothing. The cars caught fire. The flames and smoke shot up into the air. The wounded began to groan and, without waiting for the flesh to roast, I darted like a flash into the field. What a leap!

Fortunately the low hills of the Roman Campagna are very convenient for this kind of sport and I was no means behind in the line of runners. When, out of breath, I hurled myself upon the ground, it was no longer possible to hear or see anything. Only Toppi was approaching. But what a terrible thing this heart is! My face touched the earth. The earth was cool, firm, calm and here I liked it. It seemed as if it had restored my breath and put my heart back into its place. I felt easier. The stars above were calm. There was nothing for them to get excited about. They were not concerned with things below. They merely shine in triumph. That is their eternal ball. And at this brilliant ball the earth, clothed in darkness, appeared as an enchanting stranger in a black mask. (Not at all badly expressed? I trust that you, my reader, will be pleased: my style and my manners are improving!)

I kissed Toppi in the darkness. I always kiss those I like in the darkness. And I said:

"You are carrying your human form, Toppi, very well. I respect you. But what are we to do now? Those lights yonder in the sky—they are the lights of Rome. But they are too far away!"

"Yes, it is Rome," affirmed Toppi, and raised his hand: "do you hear whistling?"

From somewhere in the distance came the long-drawn, piercing, shrieking of locomotives. They were sounding the alarm.

"Yes, they are whistling," I said and laughed.

"They are whistling!" repeated Toppi smiling. He never laughs.

But here again I began to feel uncomfortable. I was cold, lonely, quivering. In my feet there was still the sensation of treading upon corpses. I wanted to shake myself like a dog after a bath. You must understand me: it was the first time that I had seen and felt your corpse, my dear reader, and if you pardon me, it did not appeal to me at all. Why did it not protest when I walked over its face? George had such a beautiful young face and he carried himself with much dignity. Remember your face, too, may be trod upon. And will you, too, remain submissive?

We did not proceed to Rome but went instead in search of the nearest night lodging. We walked long. We grew tired. We longed to drink, oh, how we longed to drink! And now, permit me to present to you my new friend, Signor Thomas Magnus and his beautiful daughter, Maria.

At first we observed the faint flicker of a light. As we approached nearer we found a little house, its white walls gleaming through a thicket of dark cypress trees and shrubbery. There was a light in one of the windows, the rest were barricaded with shutters. The house had a stone fence, an iron gate, strong doors. And—silence. At first glance it all looked suspicious. Toppi knocked. Again silence. I knocked. Still silence. Finally there came a gruff voice, asking from behind the iron door:

"Who are you? What do you want?"

Hardly mumbling with his parched tongue, my brave Toppi narrated the story of the catastrophe and our escape. He spoke at length and then came the click of a lock and the door was opened. Following behind our austere and silent stranger we entered the house, passed through several dark and silent rooms, walked up a flight of creaking stairs into a brightly lighted room, apparently the stranger's workroom. There was much light, many books, with one open beneath a low lamp shaded by a simple, green globe. We had not noticed this light in the field. But what astonished me was the silence of the house. Despite the rather early hour not a move, not a sound, not a voice was to be heard.

"Have a seat."

We sat down and Toppi, now almost in pain, began again to narrate his story. But the strange host interrupted him:

"Yes, a catastrophe. They often occur on our roads. Were there many victims?"

Toppi continued his prattle and the host, while listening to him, took a revolver out of his pocket and hid it in a table drawer, adding carelessly:

"This is not—a particularly quiet neighborhood. Well, please, remain here."

For the first time he raised his dark eyebrows and his large dim eyes and studied us intently as if he were gazing upon something savage in a museum. It was an impolite and brazen stare. I arose and said:

"I fear that we are not welcome here, Signor, and——"

He stopped Me with an impatient and slightly sarcastic gesture.

"Nonsense, you remain here. I will get you some wine and food. My servant is here in the daytime only, so allow me to wait on you. You will find the bathroom behind this door. Go wash and freshen up while I get the wine. Make yourself at home."

While we ate and drank—with savage relish, I confess—this unsympathetic gentleman kept on reading a book as if there were no one else in the room, undisturbed by Toppi's munching and the dog's struggle with a bone. I studied my host carefully. Almost my height, his pale face bore an expression of weariness. He had a black, oily, bandit-like beard. But his brow was high and his nose betrayed good sense. How would you describe it? Well, here again I seek comparisons. Imagine the nose betraying the story of a great, passionate, extraordinary, secret life. It is beautiful and seems to have been made not out of muscle and cartilage, but out of—what do you call it?—out of thoughts and brazen desires. He seems quite brave too. But I was particularly attracted by his hands: very big, very white and giving the impression of self-control. I do not know why his hands attracted me so much. But suddenly I thought: how beautifully exact the number of fingers, exactly ten of them, ten thin, evil, wise, crooked fingers!

I said politely:

"Thank you, signor——"

He replied:

"My name is Magnus. Thomas Magnus. Have some wine? Americans?"

I waited for Toppi to introduce me, according to the English custom, and I looked toward Magnus. One had to be an ignorant, illiterate animal not to know me.

Toppi broke in:

"Mr. Henry Wondergood of Illinois. His secretary, Irwin Toppi, your obedient servant. Yes, citizens of the United States."

The old buffoon blurted out his tirade, evincing a thorough lack of pride, and Magnus—yes, he was a little startled. Billions, my friend, billions. He gazed at Me long and intently:

"Mr. Wondergood? Henry Wondergood? Are you not, sir, that American billionaire who seeks to bestow upon humanity the benefits of his billions?"

I modestly shook my head in the affirmative.

"Yes, I am the gentleman."

Toppi shook his head in affirmation—the ass:

"Yes, we are the gentlemen."

Magnus bowed and said with a tinge of irony in his voice:

"Humanity is awaiting you, Mr. Wondergood. Judging by the Roman newspapers it is extremely impatient. But I must crave your pardon for this very modest meal: I did not know...."

I seized his large, strangely warm hand and shaking it violently, in American fashion, I said:

"Nonsense, Signor Magnus. I was a swine-herd before I became a billionaire, while you are a straightforward, honest and noble gentleman, whose hand I press with the utmost respect. The devil take it, not a single human face has yet aroused in me as much sympathy as yours!"

Magnus said....

Magnus said nothing! I cannot continue this: "I said," "he said,"—This cursed consistency is deadly to my inspiration. It transforms me into a silly romanticist of a boulevard sheet and makes me lie like a mediocrity. I have five senses. I am a complete human being and yet I speak only of the hearing. And how about the sight? I assure you it did not remain idle. And this sensation of the earth, of Italy, of My existence which I now perceive with a new and sweet strength! You imagine that all I did was to listen to wise Thomas Magnus. He speaks and I gaze, understand, answer, while I think: what a beautiful earth, what a beautiful Campagna di Roma! I persisted in penetrating the recesses of the house, into its locked silent rooms. With every moment my joy mounted at the thought that I am alive, that I can speak and play and, suddenly, I rather liked the idea of being human.

I remember that I held out my card to Magnus. "Henry Wondergood." He was surprised, but laid the card politely on the table. I felt like implanting a kiss on his brow for this politeness, for the fact that he too was human. I, too, am human. I was particularly proud of my foot encased in a fine, tan leather shoe and I persisted in swinging it: swing on beautiful, human, American foot! I was extremely emotional that evening! I even wanted to weep: to look my host straight in the eyes and to squeeze out of my own eyes, so full of love and goodness, two little tears. I actually did it, for at that moment I felt a little pleasant sting in my nose, as if it had been hit by a spurt of lemonade. I observed that my two little tears made an impression upon Magnus.

But Toppi!—While I experienced this wondrous poem of feeling human and even of weeping,—he slept like a dead one at the very same table. I was rather angered. This was really going too far. I wanted to shout at him, but Magnus restrained me:

"He has had a good deal of excitement and is weary, Mr. Wondergood."

The hour had really grown late. We had been talking and arguing with Magnus for two hours when Toppi fell asleep. I sent him off to bed while we continued to talk and drink for quite a while. I drank more wine, but Magnus restrained himself. There was a dimness about his face. I was beginning to develop an admiration for his grim and, at times, evil, secretive countenance. He said:

"I believe in your altruistic passion, Mr. Wondergood. But I do not believe that you, a man of wisdom and of action, and, it seems to me, somewhat cold, could place any serious hopes upon your money——"

"Three billion dollars—that is a mighty power, Magnus!"

"Yes, three billion dollars, a mighty power, indeed," he agreed, rather unwillingly—"but what will you do with it?"

I laughed.

"You probably want to say what can this ignoramus of an American, this erstwhile swine-herd, who knows swine better than he knows men, do with the money?"

"The first business helps the other," said Magnus.

"I dare say you have but a slight opinion of this foolish philanthropist whose head has been turned by his gold," said I. "Yes, to be sure, what can I do? I can open another university in Chicago, or another maternity hospital in San Francisco, or another humanitarian reformatory in New York."

"The latter would be a distinct work of mercy," quoth Magnus. "Do not gaze at me with such reproach, Mr. Wondergood: I am not jesting. You will find in me the same pure love for humanity which burns so fiercely in you."

He was laughing at me and I felt pity for him: not to love people! Miserable, unfortunate Magnus. I could kiss his brow with great pleasure! Not to love people!

"Yes, I do not love them," affirmed Magnus, "but I am glad that you do not intend to travel the conventional road of all American philanthropists. Your billions——"

"Three billions, Magnus! One could build a nation on this money——"

"Yes?——"

"Or destroy a nation," said I. "With this gold, Magnus, one can start a war or a revolution——"

"Yes?——"

I actually succeeded in arousing his interest: his large white hands trembled slightly and in his eyes there gleamed for a moment a look of respect: "You, Wondergood, are not as foolish as I thought!" He arose, paced up and down the room, and halting before me asked sneeringly:

"And you know exactly what your humanity needs most: the creation of a new or the destruction of the old state? War or peace? Rest or revolution? Who are you, Mr. Wondergood of Illinois, that you essay to solve *these* problems? You had better keep on building your maternity hospitals and universities. That is far less dangerous work."

I liked the man's hauteur. I bowed my head modestly and said:

"You are right, Signor Magnus. Who am I, Henry Wondergood, to undertake the solution of these problems? But I do not intend to solve them. I merely indicate them. I indicate them and I seek the solution. I seek the solution and the man who can give it to me. I have never read a serious book carefully. I see you have quite a supply of books here. You are a misanthrope, Magnus. You are too much of a European not to be easily disillusioned in things, while we, young America, believe in humanity. A man must be created. You in Europe are bad craftsmen and have created a bad man. We shall create a better one. I beg your pardon for my frankness. As long as I was merely Henry Wondergood I devoted myself only to the creation of pigs—and my pigs, let me say to you, have been awarded no fewer medals and decorations than Field Marshal Moltke. But now I desire to create people."

Magnus smiled:

"You are an alchemist, Wondergood: you would transform lead into gold!"

"Yes, I want to create gold and I seek the philosopher's stone. But has it not already been found? It has been found, only you do not know how to use it: It is love. Ah, Magnus, I do not know yet what I will do, but my plans are heroic and magnificent. If not for that misanthropic smile of yours I might go further. Believe in Man, Magnus, and give me your aid. You know what Man needs most."

He said coldly and with sadness:

"He needs prisons and gallows."

I exclaimed in anger (I am particularly adept in feigning anger):

"You are slandering me, Magnus! I see that you must have experienced some very great misfortune, perhaps treachery and——"

"Hold on, Wondergood! I never speak of myself and do not like to hear others speak of me. Let it be sufficient for you to know that you are the first man in four years to break in upon my solitude and this only due to chance. I do not like people."

"Oh, pardon. But I do not believe it."

Magnus went over to the bookcase and with an expression of supreme contempt he seized the first volume he laid his hands upon.

"And you who have read no books," he said, "do you know what these books are about? Only about evil, about the mistakes and sufferings of humanity. They are filled with tears and blood, Wondergood. Look: in this thin little book which I clasp between two fingers is contained a whole ocean of human blood, and if you should take all of them together——. And who has spilled this blood? The devil?"

I felt flattered and wanted to bow in acknowledgment, but he threw the book aside and shouted:

"No, sir: Man! Man has spilled this blood! Yes, I do read books but only for one purpose; to learn how to hate man and to hold him in contempt. You, Wondergood, have transformed your pigs into gold, yes? And I can see how your gold is being transformed back again into pigs. They will devour you, Wondergood. But I do not wish either to prattle or to lie: Throw your money into the sea or—build some new prisons and gallows. You are vain like all men. Then go on building gallows. You will be respected by serious people, while the flock in general will call you great. Or, don't you, American from Illinois, want to get into the Pantheon?"

"No, Magnus!——"

"Blood!" cried Magnus. "Can't you see that it is everywhere? Here it is on your boot now——"

I confess that at the moment Magnus appeared to be insane. I jerked my foot in sudden fear and only then did I perceive a dark, reddish spot on my shoe—how dastardly!

Magnus smiled and immediately regaining his composure continued calmly and without emotion:

"I have unwittingly startled you, Mr. Wondergood? Nonsense! You probably stepped on something inadvertently. A mere trifle. But this conversation, a conversation I have not conducted for a number of years, makes me uneasy and—good night, Mr. Wondergood. To-morrow I shall have the honor of presenting you to my daughter, and now you will permit me——"

And so on. In short, this gentleman conducted me to my room in a most impolite manner and well nigh put me to bed. I offered no resistance: why should I? I must say that I did not like him at this moment. I was even pleased when he turned to go but, suddenly, he turned at the very threshold and stepping forward, stretched out his large white hands.

And murmured:

"Do you see these hands? There is blood on them! Let it be the blood of a scoundrel, a torturer, a tyrant, but it is the same, red human blood. Good night!"

—He spoiled my night for me. I swear by eternal salvation that on that night I felt great pleasure in being a man, and I made myself thoroughly at home in his narrow human skin. It made me feel uncomfortable in the armpits. You see, I bought it ready made and thought that it would be as comfortable as if it had been made to measure! I was highly emotional. I was extremely good and affable. I was very eager to play, but I was not inclined to tragedy! Blood! How can any person of good breeding thrust his white hands under the nose of a stranger—Hangmen have very white hands!

Do not think I am jesting. I did not feel well. In the daytime I still manage to subdue Wondergood but at night he lays his hands upon me. It is he who fills me with his silly dreams and shakes within me his entire dusty archive—And how godlessly silly and meaningless are his dreams! He fusses about within me all night long like a returned master, seems to be looking about for something, grumbles about losses and wear and tear and sneezes and cavorts about like a dog lying uncomfortable on its bed. It is he who draws me in at night like a mass of wet lime into the depths of miserable humanity, where I nearly choke to death. When I awake in the morning I feel that Wondergood has infused ten more degrees of human into me—Think of it: He may soon eject me all together and leave me standing outside—he, the miserable owner of an empty barn into which I brought breath and soul!

Like a hurried thief I crawled into a stranger's clothes, the pockets of which are bulging with forged promissory notes—no, still worse!

It is not only uncomfortable attire. It is a low, dark and stifling jail, wherein I occupy less space than a ring might in the stomach of Wondergood. You, my dear reader, have been hidden in your prison from childhood and you even seem to like it, but I—I come from the kingdom of liberty. And I refuse to be Wondergood's tape worm: one swallow of poison and I am free again. What will you say then, scoundrel Wondergood? Without me you will be devoured by the worms. You will crack open at the seams—Miserable carcass! touch me not!

On this night however I was in the absolute power of Wondergood. What is human blood to Me? What do I care about the troubles of *their* life! But Wondergood was quite aroused by the crazy Magnus. Suddenly I felt—just think of it—! That I am filled with blood, like the bladder of an ox, and the bladder is very thin and weak, so that it would be dangerous to prick it. Prick it and out spurts the blood! I was terrified at the idea that I might be killed in this house: That some one might cut my throat and turning me upside down, hanging by the legs, would let the blood run out upon the floor.

I lay in the darkness and strained my ears to hear whether or not Magnus was approaching with his white hands. And the greater the silence in this cursed house the more terrified I grew. Even Toppi failed to snore as usual. This made me angry. Then my body began to ache. Perhaps I was injured in the wreck, or was it weariness brought on by the flight? Then my body began to itch in the most ordinary way and I even began to move the feet: it was the appearance of the jovial clown in the tragedy!

Suddenly a dream seized Me by the feet and dragged me rapidly below. I hardly had time enough to shout. And what nonsense arose before me! Do you ever have such dreams? I felt that I was a bottle of champagne, with a thin neck and sealed, but filled not with wine but with blood! And it seemed that not only I but all people had become bottles with sealed tops and all of us were arranged in a row on a seashore. And, Someone horrible was approaching from Somewhere and wanted to smash us all. And I saw how foolish it would be to do so and wanted to shout: "Don't smash them. Get a corkscrew!" But I had no voice. I was a bottle. Suddenly the dead lackey George approached. In his hands was a huge sharp corkscrew. He said something and seized me by the throat—Ah, ah, by the throat!——

I awoke in pain. Apparently he did try to open me up. My wrath was so great that I neither sighed nor smiled nor moved. I simply killed Wondergood again. I gnashed my teeth, straightened out my eyes, closed them calmly, stretched out at full length and lay peacefully in the full consciousness of the greatness of my Ego. Had the ocean itself moved up on me I would not have batted an eye! Get thee hence, my friend, I wish to be alone.

And the body grew silent, colorless, airy and empty again. With light step I left it and before my eyes there arose a vision of the *extra-ordinary*, that which cannot be expressed in your language, my poor friend! Satisfy your curiosity with the dream I have just confided to you and ask no more! Or does not the "huge, sharp corkscrew" suit you? But it is so—artistic!

***

In the morning I was well again, refreshed and beautiful. I yearned for the play, like an actor who has just left his dressing room. Of course I did not forget to shave. This canaille Wondergood gets overgrown with hair as quickly as his golden skinned pigs. I complained about this to Toppi with whom, while waiting for Magnus, I was walking in the garden. And Toppi, thinking a while, replied philosophically:

"Yes, man sleeps and his beard grows. This is as it should be—for the barbers!"

Magnus appeared. He was no more hospitable than yesterday and his pale face carried unmistakable indications of weariness. But he was calm and polite. How black his beard is in the daytime! He pressed my hand in cold politeness and said: (we were perched on a wall.)

"You are enjoying the Roman Campagna, Mr. Wondergood? A magnificent sight! It is said that the Campagna is noted for its fevers, but there is but one fever it produces in me—the fever of thought!"

Apparently Wondergood did not have much of a liking for nature, and I have not yet managed to develop a taste for earthly landscape: an empty field for me. I cast my eyes politely over the countryside before us and said:

"People interest me more, Signor Magnus."

He gazed at me intently with his dark eyes and lowering his voice said dryly and with apparent reluctance:

"Just two words about people, Mr. Wondergood. You will soon see my daughter, Maria. She is my three billions. You understand?"

I nodded my head in approval.

"But your California does not produce such gold. Neither does any other country on this dirty earth. It is the gold of the heavens. I am not a believer, Mr. Wondergood, but even I experience some doubts when I meet the gaze of my Maria. Hers are the only hands into which you might without the slightest misgiving place your billions——"

I am an old bachelor and I was overcome with fear, but Magnus continued sternly with a ring of triumph in his voice:

"But she will not accept them, Sir! Her gentle hands must never touch this golden dirt. Her clean eyes will never behold any sight but that of this endless, godless Campagna. Here is her monastery, Mr. Wondergood, and there is but one exit for her from here: into the Kingdom of Heaven, if it does exist!"

"I beg your pardon but I cannot understand this, my dear Magnus!" I protested in great joy. "Life and people——"

The face of Thomas Magnus grew angry, as it did yesterday, and in stern ridicule, he interrupted me:

"And I beg you to grasp, *dear* Wondergood, that life and people are not for Maria. It is enough that I know them. My duty was to *warn* you. And now"—he again assumed the attitude of cold politeness—"I ask you to come to my table. You too, Mr. Toppi!"

We had begun to eat, and were chattering of small matters, when

Maria entered. The door through which she entered was behind my back. I mistook her soft step for those of the maid carrying the dishes, but I was astonished by the long-nosed Toppi, sitting opposite me. His eyes grew round like circles, his face red, as if he were choking. His Adam's apple seemed to be lifted above his neck as if driven by a wave, and to disappear again somewhere behind his narrow, ministerial collar. Of course, I thought he was choking to death with a fishbone and shouted:

"Toppi! What is the matter with you? Take some water."

But Magnus was already on his feet, announcing coldly:

"My daughter, Maria. Mr. Henry Wondergood!"

I turned about quickly and—how can I express the extraordinary when it is inexpressible? It was something more than beautiful. It was terrible in its beauty. I do not want to seek comparisons. I shall leave that to you. Take all that you have ever seen or ever known of the beautiful on earth: the lily, the stars, the sun, but add, add still more. But not this was the awful aspect of it: There was something else: the elusive yet astonishing similarity—to whom? Whom have I met upon this earth who was so beautiful—so beautiful and awe-inspiring—awe-inspiring and unapproachable. I have learned by this time your entire archive, Wondergood, and I do not believe that it comes from your modest gallery!

"Madonna!" mumbled Toppi in a hoarse voice, scared out of his wits.

So that is it! Yes, Madonna. The fool was right, and I, Satan, could understand his terror. Madonna, whom people see only in churches, in paintings, in the imagination of artists. Maria, the name which rings only in hymns and prayer books, heavenly beauty, mercy, forgiveness and love! Star of the Seas! Do you like that name: Star of the Seas?

It was really devilishly funny. I made a deep bow and almost blurted out:

"Madam, I beg pardon for my unbidden intrusion, but I really did not expect to meet you *here*. I most humbly beg your pardon, but I could not imagine that this black bearded fellow has the honor of having you for his daughter. A thousand times I crave your pardon for——"

But enough. I said something else.

"How do you do, Signorina. It is indeed a pleasure."

And she really did not indicate in any way that she was *already* acquainted with Me. One must respect an incognito if one would remain a gentleman and only a scoundrel would dare to tear a mask from a lady's face! This would have been all the more impossible, because her father, Thomas Magnus, continued to urge us with a chuckle:

"Do eat, please, Mr. Toppi. Why do you not drink, Mr. Wondergood? The wine is splendid."

In the course of what followed:

1. She breathed— 2. She blinked— 3. She ate—and she was a beautiful girl, about eighteen years of age, and her dress was white and her throat bare. It was really laughable. I gazed at her bare neck and—believe me, my earthly friend: I am not easily seduced, I am not a romantic youth, but I am not old by any means, I am not at all bad looking, I enjoy an independent position in the world and—don't you like the combination: Satan and *Maria*? *Maria* and Satan! In evidence of the seriousness of my intentions I can submit at that moment I thought more of *our* descendants and sought a name for *our* first-born than indulged in frivolity.

Suddenly Toppi's Adam's apple gave a jerk and he inquired hoarsely:

"Has any one ever painted your portrait, Signorina?"

"Maria never poses for painters!" broke in Magnus sternly. I felt like laughing at the fool Toppi. I had already opened wide my mouth, filled with a set of first-class American teeth, when Maria's pure gaze pierced my eyes and everything flew to the devil,—as in that moment of the railway catastrophe! You understand: she turned me inside out, like a stocking—or how shall I put it? My fine Parisian costume was driven inside of me and my still finer thoughts which, however, I would not have wanted to convey to the lady, suddenly appeared upon the surface. With all my secrecy I was left no more sealed than a room in a fifteen cent lodging house.

But she *forgave* me, said nothing and threw her gaze like a projector in the direction of Toppi, illumining his entire body. You, too, would have laughed had you seen how this poor old devil was set aglow and aflame by this gaze—clear from the prayer book to the fishbone with which he nearly choked to death.

Fortunately for both of us Magnus arose and invited us to follow him into the garden.

"Come, let us go into the garden," said he. "Maria will show you her favorite flowers."

Yes, Maria! But seek no songs of praise from me, oh poet! I was mad! I was as provoked as a man whose closet has just been ransacked by a burglar. I wanted to gaze at Maria but was compelled to look upon the foolish flowers—because I dared not lift my eyes. I am a gentleman and cannot appear before a lady without a necktie. I was seized by a curious humility. Do you like to feel humble? I do not.

I do not know what Maria said. But I swear by eternal salvation—her gaze, and her entire uncanny countenance was the embodiment of an all-embracing meaning so that any wise word I might have uttered would have sounded meaningless. The wisdom of words is necessary only for those poor in spirit. The right are silent. Take note of that, little poet, sage and eternal chatterbox, wherever you may be. Let it be sufficient for you that I have humbled myself to speak.

Ah, but I have forgotten my humility! She walked and I and Toppi crawled after her. I detested myself and this broad-backed Toppi because of his hanging nose and large, pale ears. What was needed here was an Apollo and not a pair of ordinary Americans.

We felt quite relieved when she had gone and we were left alone with Magnus. It was all so sweet and simple! Toppi abandoned his religious airs and I crossed my legs comfortably, lit a cigar, and fixed my steel-sharp gaze upon the whites of Magnus's eyes.

"You must be off to Rome, Mr. Wondergood. They are probably worrying about you," said our host in a tone of loving concern.

"I can send Toppi," I replied. He smiled and added ironically:

"I hardly think that would be sufficient, Mr. Wondergood!"

I sought to clasp his great white hand but it did not seem to move closer. But I caught it just the same, pressed it warmly and he was compelled to return the pressure!

"Very well, Signor Magnus! I am off at once!" I said.

"I have already sent for the carriage," he replied. "Is not the Campagna beautiful in the morning?"

I again took a polite look at the country-side and said with emotion:

"Yes, it is beautiful! Irwin, my friend, leave us for a moment. I have a few words to say to Signor Magnus——"

Toppi left and Signor Magnus opened wide his big sad eyes. I again tried my steel on him, and bending forward closer to his dark face, I asked:

"Have you ever observed *dear* Magnus, the very striking resemblance between your daughter, the Signorina Maria, and a certain—celebrated personage? Don't you think she resembles the Madonna?"

"Madonna?" drawled out Magnus. "No, *dear* Wondergood, I haven't noticed that. I never go to church. But I fear you will be late. The Roman fever——"

I again seized his white hand and shook it vigorously. No, I did not tear it off. And from my eyes there burst forth again *those* two tears:

"Let us speak plainly, Signor Magnus," said I. "I am a straightforward man and have grown to love you. Do you want to come along with me and be the lord of my billions?"

Magnus was silent. His hand lay motionless in mine. His eyes were lowered and something dark seemed to pass over his face, then immediately to disappear. Finally he said, seriously and simply:

"I understand you, Mr. Wondergood—but I must refuse. No, I will not go with you. I have failed to tell you one thing, but your frankness and confidence in me compels me to say that I must, to a certain extent, steer clear of the police."

"The Roman police," I asked, betraying a slight excitement. "Nonsense, we shall buy it."

"No, the international," he replied. "I hope you do not think that I have committed some base crime. The trouble is not with police which can be bought. You are right, Mr. Wondergood, when you say that one can buy almost any one. The truth is that I can be of no use to you. What do you want me for? You love humanity and I detest it. At best I am indifferent to it. Let it live and not interfere with me. Leave me my Maria, leave me the right and strength to detest people as I read the history of their life. Leave me my Campagna and that is all I want and all of which I am capable. All the oil within me has burned out, Wondergood. You see before you an extinguished lamp hanging on a wall, a lamp which once—Goodbye."

"I do not ask your confidence, Magnus," I interjected.

"Pardon me, you will never receive it, Mr. Wondergood. My name is an invention but it is the only one I can offer to my friends."

To tell the truth: I liked "Thomas Magnus" at that moment. He spoke bravely and simply. In his face one could read stubbornness and will. This man knew the value of human life and had the mien of one condemned to death. But it was the mien of a proud, uncompromising criminal, who will never accept the ministrations of a priest! For a moment I thought: My Father had many bastard children, deprived of legacy and wandering about the world. Perhaps Thomas Magnus is one of these wanderers? And is it possible that I have met a *brother* on this earth? Very interesting. But from a purely human, business point of view, one cannot help but respect a man whose hands are steeped in blood!

I saluted, changed my position, and in the humblest possible manner, asked Magnus's permission to visit him occasionally and seek his advice. He hesitated but finally looked me straight in the face and agreed.

"Very well, Mr. Wondergood. You may come. I hope to hear from you things that may supplement the knowledge I glean from my books. And, by the way, Mr. Toppi has made an excellent impression upon my Maria"——

"Toppi?"

"Yes. She has found a striking resemblance between him and one of her favorite saints. She goes to church frequently."

Toppi a saint! Or has his prayer book overbalanced his huge back and the fishbone in his throat. Magnus gazed at me almost gently and only his thin nose seemed to tremble slightly with restrained laughter.— It is very pleasant to know that behind this austere exterior there is so much quiet and restrained merriment!

It was twilight when we left. Magnus followed us to the threshold, but Maria remained in seclusion. The little white house surrounded by the cypress trees was as quiet and silent as we found it yesterday, but the silence was of a different character: the silence was the soul of Maria.

I confess that I felt rather sad at this departure but very soon came a new series of impressions, which dispelled this feeling. We were approaching Rome. We entered the brightly illuminated, densely populated streets through some opening in the city wall and the first thing we saw in the Eternal City was a creaking trolley car, trying to make its way through the same hole in the wall. Toppi, who was acquainted with Rome, revelled in the familiar atmosphere of the churches we were passing and indicated with his long finger the *remnants* of ancient Rome which seemed to be clinging to the huge wall of the new structures: just as if the latter had been bombarded with the shells of old and fragments of the missiles had clung to the bricks.

Here and there we came upon additional heaps of this old rubbish. Above a low parapet of stone, we observed a dark shallow ditch and a large triumphal gate, half sunk in the earth. "The Forum!" exclaimed Toppi, majestically. Our coachman nodded his head in affirmation. With every new pile of old stone and brick the fellow swelled with pride, while I longed for my New York and its skyscrapers, and tried to calculate the number of trucks that would be necessary to clear these heaps of rubbish called ancient Rome away before morning. When I mentioned this to Toppi he was insulted and replied:

"You don't understand anything: better close your eyes and just reflect that you are in Rome."

I did so and was again convinced that sight is as much of an impediment to the mind as sound: not without reason are all wise folk on the earth blind and all good musicians deaf.

Like Toppi I began to sniff the air and through my sense of smell I gathered more of Rome and its horribly long and highly entertaining history than hitherto: thus a decaying leaf in the woods smells stronger than the young and green foliage. Will you believe me when I say that I sensed the odor of blood and Nero? But when I opened my eyes expectantly I observed a plain, everyday kiosk and a lemonade stand.

"Well, how do you like it?" growled Toppi, still dissatisfied.

"It smells——"

"Well, certainly it smells! It will smell stronger with every hour:

these are old, strong aromas, Mr. Wondergood."

And so it really was: the odor grew in strength. I cannot find comparisons to make it clear to you. All the sections of my brain began to move and buzz like bees aroused by smoke. It is strange, but it seems that Rome is included in the archive of the silly Wondergood. Perhaps this is his native town? When we approached a certain populous square I sensed the clear odor of some blood relatives, which was soon followed by the conviction that I, too, have walked these streets before. Have I, like Toppi, previously donned the human form? Ever louder buzzed the bees. My entire beehive buzzed and suddenly thousands of faces, dim and white, beautiful and horrible, began to dance before me; thousands upon thousands of voices, noises, cries, laughters and sighs nearly set me deaf. No, this was no longer a beehive: it was a huge, fiery smithy, where firearms were being forged with the red sparks flying all about. Iron!

Of course, if I had lived in Rome before, I must have been one of its emperors: I *remember* the expression of my face. I remember the movement of my bare neck as I turn my head. I remember the touch of golden laurels upon my bald head—Iron! Ah, I hear the steps of the iron legions of Rome. I hear the iron voices: "Vivat Cæsar!"

I am hot. I am burning. Or was I not an emperor but simply one of the "victims" when Rome burned down in accordance with the magnificent plan of Nero? No, this is not a fire. This is a funeral pyre on which I am forcibly esconsced. I hear the snake-like hissing of the tongues of flame beneath my feet. I strain my neck, all lined with blue veins, and in my throat there rises the final curse—or blessing? Think of it: I even remember that Roman face in the front row of spectators, which even then gave me no rest because of its idiotic expression and sleepy eyes: I am being burned and it sleeps!

"Hotel 'Internationale'"—cried Toppi, and I opened my eyes.

We were going up a hill along a quiet street, at the end of which there glowed a large structure, worthy even of New York: it was the hotel where we had previously wired for reservations. They probably thought we had perished in the wreck. My funeral pyre was extinguished. I grew as merry as a darkey who has just escaped from hard labor and I whispered to Toppi:

"Well, Toppi, and how about the Madonna?"

"Y-yes, interesting. I was frightened at first and nearly choked to death——"

"With a bone? You are silly, Toppi: she is polite and did not recognize you. She simply took you for one of her saints. It is a pity, old boy, that we have chosen for ourselves these solemn, American faces: had we looked around more carefully we might have found some more beautiful."

"I am quite satisfied with mine," said Toppi sadly, and turned away. A glow of secret self-satisfaction appeared upon his long, shiny nose. Ah, Toppi, Ah, the saint!

But we were already being accorded a triumphal reception.

February 14. Rome, Hotel "Internationale."
I do not want to go to Magnus. I am thinking too much of his Madonna of flesh and bone. I have come here to lie and to play merrily and I am not at all taken by the prospect of being a mediocre actor, who weeps behind the scenes and appears on the stage with his eyes perfectly dry. Moreover, I have no time to gad about the fields catching butterflies with a net like a boy.

The whole of Rome is buzzing about me. I am an extraordinary man, who loves his fellow beings and I am celebrated. The mobs who flock to worship Me are no less numerous than those who worship the Vicar of Christ himself, two Popes all at once.—Yes, happy Rome cannot consider itself an orphan!

I am now living at the hotel, where all is aquiver with ecstacy when I put my shoes outside my door for the night, but they are renovating a palace for me: the historic Villa Orsini. Painters, sculptors and poets are kept busy. One brush-pusher is already painting my portrait, assuring me that I remind him of one of the Medicis. The other brush-pushers are sharpening their knives for him.

I ask him:

"And can you paint a Madonna?"

Certainly he can. It was he, if the signor recollects, who painted the famous Turk on the cigarette boxes, the Turk whose fame is known even in America. And now three brush-pushers are painting Madonnas for me. The rest are running about Rome seeking models. I said to one, in my barbarous, American ignorance of the higher arts:

"But if you find such a model, Signor, just bring her to me. Why waste paint and canvas?"

He was evidently pained and mumbled:

"Ah, Signor—a model?"

I think he took me for a merchant in "live stock." But, fool, why do I need your aid for which I must pay a commission, when my ante-chamber is filled with a flock of beauties? They all worship me. I remind them of Savanarola, and they seek to transform every dark corner in my drawing room, and every soft couch into a confessional. I am so glad that these society ladies, like the painters, know so well the history of their country and realize who I am.

The joy of the Roman papers on finding that I did not perish in the wreck and lost neither my legs nor my billions, was equal to the joy of the papers of Jerusalem on the day of the resurrection of Christ—in reality there was little cause for satisfaction on the part of the latter, as far as I am able to read history. I feared that I might remind the journalists of J. Cæsar, but fortunately they think little of the past and confined themselves to pointing out my resemblance to President Wilson. Scoundrels! They were simply flattering my American patriotism. To the majority, however, I recall a Prophet, but they do not know which one. On this point they are modestly silent. At any rate it is not Mahomet: my opposition to marriage is well known at all telegraph stations.

It is difficult to imagine the filth on which I fed my hungry interviewers. Like an experienced swine-herd, I gaze with horror on the mess they feed upon. They eat and yet they live. Although, I must admit, I do not see them growing fat! Yesterday morning I flew in an aeroplane over Rome and the Campagna. You will probably ask whether I saw Maria's home? No. I did not find it: how can one find a grain of sand among a myriad of other grains—But I really did not look for it: I felt horror-stricken at the great altitude.

But my good interviewers, restless and impatient, were astounded by my coolness and courage. One fellow, strong, surly and bearded, who reminded me of Hannibal, was the first to reach me after the flight, and asked:

"Did not the sensation of flying in the air, Mr. Wondergood, the feeling of having conquered the elements, thrill you with a sense of pride in man, who has subdued——"

He repeated the question: they don't seem to trust me, somehow, and are always suggesting the proper answers. But I shrugged my shoulders and exclaimed sadly:

"Can you imagine Signor—No! Only once did I have a sense of pride in men and that was—in the lavatory on board the 'Atlantic.'"

"Oh! In the lavatory! But what happened? A storm, and you were astounded by the genius of man, who has subdued——"

"Nothing extraordinary happened. But I was astounded by the genius of man who managed to create a palace out of such a disgusting necessity as a lavatory."

"Oh!"

"A real temple, in which one is the arch priest!"

"Permit me to make a note of that. It is such an original—illumination of the problem——"

And to-day the whole Eternal City was feeding on this sally. Not only did they not request me to leave the place, but on the contrary, this was the day of the first official visits to my apartments: something on the order of a minister of state, an ambassador or some other palace chef came and poured sugar and cinnamon all over me as if I were a pudding. Later in the day I returned the visits: it is not very pleasant to keep such things.

Need I say that I have a nephew? Every American millionaire has a nephew in Europe. My nephew's name is also Wondergood. He is connected with some legation, is very correct in manners and his bald spot is so oiled that my kiss could serve me as a breakfast were I fond of scented oil. But one must be willing to sacrifice something, especially the gratification of a sense of smell. The kiss cost me not a cent, while it meant a great deal to the young man. It opened for him a wide credit on soap and perfumery.

But enough! When I look at these ladies and gentlemen and reflect that they are just as they were at the court of Aschurbanipal and that for the past 2000 years the pieces of silver received by Judas continue to bear interest, like his kiss—I grow bored with this old and threadbare play. Ah, I want a great play. I seek originality and talent. I want beautiful lines and bold strokes. This company here casts me in the rôle of an old brass band conductor. At times I come to the conclusion that it wasn't really worth my while to have undertaken such a long journey for the sake of this old drivel—to exchange ancient, magnificent and multi-colored Hell for its miserable replica. In truth, I am sorry that Magnus and his Madonna refused to join me—we would have played a little—just a little!

I have had but one interesting morning. In fact I was quite excited. The congregation of a so-called "free" church, composed of very serious men and women, who insist upon worshipping in accordance with the dictates of their conscience, invited Me to deliver a Sunday sermon. I donned a black frock coat, which gave me a close resemblance to—Toppi, went through a number of particularly expressive gestures before my mirror and was driven in an automobile, like a prophet—moderne, to the service. I took as my subject or "text" Jesus' advice to the rich youth to distribute his wealth among the poor—and in not more than half an hour, I demonstrated as conclusively as 2 and 2 make 4, that love of one's neighbor is the all important thing. Like a practical and careful American, however, I pointed out that it was not necessary to try and go after the whole of the kingdom of Heaven at one shot and to distribute one's wealth carelessly; that one can buy it up in lots on the instalment plan and by easy payments. The faces of the faithful bore a look of extreme concentration. They were apparently figuring out something and came to the conclusion that on the basis I suggested, the Kingdom of Heaven was attainable for the pockets of all of them.

Unfortunately, a number of my quick-witted compatriots were present in the congregation. One of them was about to rise to his feet to propose the formation of a stock company, when I realized the danger and frustrated this plan by letting loose a fountain of emotion, and thus extinguished his religiously practical zeal! What did I not talk about? I wept for my sad childhood, spent in labor and privation; I whined about my poor father who perished in a match factory. I prayed solemnly for all my brothers and sisters in Christ. The swamp I created was so huge that the journalists caught enough wild ducks to last them for six months. How we wept!

I shivered with the dampness and began to beat energetically the drum of my billions: dum-dum! Everything for others, not a cent for me: dum-dum! With a brazenness worthy of the whip I concluded "with the words of the Great Teacher:"

"Come ye unto me all who are heavy-laden and weary and I will comfort ye!"

Ah, what a pity I cannot perform miracles! A little practical miracle, something on the order of transforming a bottle of water into one of sour Chianti or some of the worshippers into pastry, would have gone a long way at that moment.—You laugh and are angry, my earthy reader? There is no reason for you to act thus. Remember only that the *extraordinary* cannot be expressed in your ventriloquist language and that my words are merely a cursed mask for my thoughts.

Maria!

You will read of my success in the newspapers. There was one fool, however, who almost spoiled my day for me: he was a member of the Salvation Army. He came to see me and suggested that I immediately take up a trumpet and lead the army into battle—they were too cheap laurels he offered and I drove him out. But Toppi—he was triumphantly silent all the way home and finally he said very respectfully:

"You were in fine mettle to-day, Mr. Wondergood. I even wept. It is a pity that neither Magnus nor his daughter heard you preach, She—she would have changed her opinion of us."

You understand, of course, that I felt like kicking this admirer out of the carriage! I again felt in the pupils of my eyes the piercing sting of hers. The speed with which I was again turned inside out and spread out on a plate for the public's view is equal only to that with which an experienced waiter opens a can of conserves. I drew my top hat over my eyes, raised the collar of my coat and looking very much like a tragedian just hissed off the stage, I rode silently, and without acknowledging the greetings showered upon me, I proceeded to my apartments. Ah, that gaze of Maria! And how could I have acknowledged the greetings when I had no cane with me?

I have declined all of to-day's invitations and am at home: I am engaged in "religious meditation"—this was how Toppi announced it to the journalists. He has really begun to respect me. Before me are whiskey and champagne. I am slowly filling up on the liquor while from the dining hall below come the distant strains of music. My Wondergood was apparently considerable of a drunkard and every night he drags me to the wineshop, to which I interpose no objection. What's the difference? Fortunately his intoxication is of a merry kind and we make quite a pleasant time of it. At first we cast our dull eyes over the furniture and involuntarily begin to calculate the value of all this bronze, these carpets, Venetian mirrors, etc.

"A trifle!" we agree, and with peculiar self-satisfaction we lose ourselves in the contemplation of our own billions, of our power and our remarkable wisdom and character. Our bliss increases with each additional glass. With peculiar pleasure we wallow in the cheap luxury of the hotel, and—think of it!—I am actually beginning to have a liking for bronze, carpets, glass and stones. My Puritan Toppi condemns luxury. It reminds him of Sodom and Gommorah. But it is difficult for me to part with these little emotional pleasures. How silly of me!

We continue to listen dully and half-heartedly to the music and venture to whistle some accompaniments. We add a little contemplation on the decollete of the ladies and then, with our step still firm, we proceed to our resting room.

But we were just ready for bed when suddenly I felt as if some one had struck me a blow and I was immediately seized with a tempest of tears, of love and sadness. The extraordinary suddenly found expression. I grew as broad as space, as deep as eternity and I embraced all in a single breath! But, oh, what sadness! Oh, what love, Maria!

But I am nothing more than a subterranean lake in the belly of Wondergood and my storms in no way disturb his firm tread. I am only a solitaire in his stomach, of which he seeks to rid himself!

We ring for the servants.

"Soda!"

I am simply drunk. Arrivederci, Signor, buona notte!

February 18, 1914. Rome, Hotel "Internationale."
Yesterday I visited Magnus. I was compelled to wait long for him, in the garden, and when he did appear he was so cold and indifferent that I felt like leaving. I observed a few gray hairs in his black beard. I had not noticed them before. Was Maria unwell? I appeared concerned. Everything here is so uncertain that on leaving a person for one hour one may have

to seek him in eternity."

"Maria is well, thank you," replied Magnus, frigidly. He seemed surprised as if my question were presumptuous and improper. "And how are your affairs, Mr. Wondergood? The Roman papers are filled with news of you. You are scoring a big success."

With pain aggravated by the absence of Maria, I revealed to Magnus my disappointment and my ennui. I spoke well, not without wit and sarcasm. I grew more and more provoked by his lack of attention and interest, plainly written on his pale and weary face. Not once did he smile or venture to put any questions, but when I reached the story of my "nephew" he frowned in displeasure and said:

"Fie! This is a cheap variety farce! How can you occupy yourself with such trifles, Mr. Wondergood?"

I replied angrily:

"But it is not I who am occupying myself with them, Signor Magnus!"

"And how about the interviews? What about that flight of yours? You should drive them away. This humbles your…three billions. And is it true that you delivered some sort of a sermon?"

The joy of play forsook me. Unwilling as Magnus was to listen to me, I told him all about my sermon and those credulous fools who swallowed sacrilege as they do marmalade.

"And did you expect anything different, Mr. Wondergood?"

"I expected that they would fall upon me with clubs for my audacity: When I sacrilegiously bandied about the words of the Testament…."

"Yes, they are beautiful words," agreed Magnus. "But didn't you know that all their worship of God and all their faith are nothing but sacrilege? When they term a wafer the body of Christ, while some Sixtus or Pius reigns undisturbed, and with the approval of all Catholics as the Vicar of Christ, why should not you, an American from Illinois, call yourself at least…his governor? This is not meant as sacrilege, Mr. Wondergood. These are simply allegories, highly convenient for blockheads, and you are only wasting your wrath. But when will you get down to *business*?"

I threw up my hands in skillfully simulated sorrow:

"I *want* to do something, but I *know* not what to do. I shall probably never get down to business until you, Magnus, agree to come to my aid."

He frowned, at his own large, motionless, white hands and then at me:

"You are too credulous, Mr. Wondergood. This is a great fault when one has three billions. No, I am of no use to you. Our roads are far apart."

"But, dear Magnus!…"

I expected him to strike me for this gentle *dear*, which I uttered in my best possible falsetto. But I ventured to continue. With all the sweetness I managed to accumulate in Rome, I looked upon the dim physiognomy of my friend and in a still gentler falsetto, I asked:

"And of what nationality are you, my *dear*…Signor Magnus? I suspect for some reason that you are not Italian?"

He replied calmly:

"No, I am not Italian."

"But where is your country?——"

"My country?… Omne solum liberam libero patria. I suppose you do not know Latin? It means: Where freedom is there is the fatherland of every free man. Will you take breakfast with me?"

The invitation was couched in such icy tones and Maria's absence was so strongly implied therein that I was compelled to decline it politely. The devil take this man! I was not at all in a merry mood that morning. I fervently wished to weep upon his breast while he mercilessly threw cold showers upon my noblest transports. I sighed and changed my pose. I assumed a pose prepared especially for Maria. Speaking in a low voice, I said:

"I want to be frank with you, Signor Magnus. My past…contains many dark pages, which I should like to redeem. I…."

He quickly interrupted me:

"There are dark pages in everybody's past, Mr. Wondergood. I myself am not so clear of reproach as to accept the confession of such a worthy gentleman."

"I am a poor spiritual father," he added with a most unpleasant laugh: "*I never pardon sinners* and, in view of that, what pleasure could there be for you in your confession. Better tell me something more about your nephew. Is he young?"

We spoke about my nephew—and Magnus smiled. A pause ensued. Then Magnus asked whether I had visited the Vatican gallery and I bade him good-by, requesting him to transmit my compliments to Maria. I confess I was a sorry sight and felt deeply indebted to Magnus when he said in bidding me farewell:

"Do not be angry with me, Mr. Wondergood. I am not altogether well to-day and…am rather worried about my affairs. That's all. I hope to be more pleasant when we meet again, but be so kind as to excuse me this morning. I shall see that Maria gets your compliments."

If this blackbearded fellow were only *playing*, I confess I would have found a worthy partner.

A dozen pickaninnies could not have licked off the honeyed expression my face assumed at Magnus' promise to transmit my greetings to Maria. All the way back to my hotel I smiled idiotically at the coachman's back and afterwards bestowed a kiss on Toppi's brow—the canaile still maintains an odor of fur, like a young devil.

"I see there was profit in your visit," said Toppi significantly. "How is Magnus'…daughter? You understand?"

"Splendid, Toppi, splendid! She said that my beauty and wisdom reminded her of Solomon's!"

Toppi smiled condescendingly at my unsuccessful jest. The honeyed expression left my face and rust and vinegar took the place of the sugar. I locked myself in my room and for a long time continued to curse Satan for falling in love with a woman.

You consider yourself original, my earthly friend, when you fall in love with a woman and begin to quiver all over with the fever of love. And I do not. I can see the legions of couples, from Adam and Eve on; I can see their kisses and caresses; I can hear the words so cursedly monotonous, and I begin to detest my own lips daring to mumble the mumbling of others, my eyes, simulating the gaze of others, my heart, surrendering obediently to the click of the lock of a house of shame. I can see all these excited animals in their groaning and their caresses and I cry with revulsion at my own mass of bones and flesh and nerves! Take care, Satan in human form, Deceit is coming over You!

Won't you take Maria for yourself, my earthly friend? Take her. She is yours, not mine. Ah, if Maria were my slave, I would put a rope around her neck and would take her, naked, to the market place: Who will buy? Who will pay the most for this unearthly beauty? Ah, do not hurt the poor blind merchant: open wide your purses, jingle louder your gold, generous gentlemen!…

What, she will not go? Fear not, Signor, she will come and she will love you…. This is simply her maidenly modesty, Sir! Shall I tie the other end of the rope about her and lead her to your bed, kind sir? Take the rope along with you. I charge nothing for that. Only rid me of this heavenly beauty! She has the face of the radiant Madonna. She is the daughter of the honorable Thomas Magnus and both of them are thieves: he stole his white hands and she—her pristine face! Ah….

But I am beginning to play with you, dear reader? That is a mistake: I have simply taken the wrong note book. No, it is not a mistake. It is worse. I play because my loneliness is very great, very deep—I fear it has no bottom at all! I stand on the edge of an abyss and hurl words, many heavy words, into it, but they fall without a sound. I hurl into it laughter, threats and moans. I spit into it. I fling into it heaps of stones and rocks. I throw mountains into it—and still it remains silent and empty. No, really, there is no bottom to this abyss and we toil in vain, you and I, my friend!

…But I see your smile and your cunning laugh: you *understand* why I spoke so sourly of loneliness…. Ah, 'tis love! And you want to ask whether I have a mistress?

Yes: there are two. One is a Russian countess. The other, an Italian countess. They differ only in the kind of perfume they use. But this is such an immaterial matter that I love them both equally.

You probably wish to ask also whether I shall ever visit Magnus again?

Yes, I shall go to Magnus. I love him very much. It matters little that his name is false and that his daughter has the audacity to resemble the Madonna. I haven't enough of Wondergood in me to be particular about a name—and I am too *human* not to forgive the efforts of others to appear *divine*.

I swear by eternal salvation that the one is worthy of the other!

February 21, 1914. Rome, Villa Orsini.

Cardinal X., the closest friend and confidante of the Pope, has paid me a visit. He was accompanied by two abbés. In general, he is a personage whose attentions to me have brought me no small measure of prestige.

I met His Eminence in the reception hall of my new palace. Toppi was dancing all about the priests, snatching their blessings quicker than a lover does the kisses of his mistress. Six devout hands hardly managed to handle one Devil, grown pious, and before we had reached the threshold of my study, he actually contrived to touch the belly of the Cardinal. What ecstasy!

Cardinal X. speaks all the European languages and, out of respect for the Stars and Stripes and my billions, he spoke English. He began the conversation by congratulating me upon the acquisition of the Villa Orsini and told me its history in detail for the past 200 years. This was quite unexpected, very long, at times confusing and unintelligible, so that I was compelled, like a real American ass, to blink constantly…but this gave me an opportunity to study my distinguished and eminent visitor.

He is not at all old. He is broad shouldered, well built and in good health. He has a large, almost square face, an olive skin, with a bluish tinge upon his shaven cheeks, and his thin, but beautiful hands reveal his Spanish blood. Before he dedicated himself to God, Cardinal X. was a Spanish grandee and duke. But his dark eyes are too small and too deeply set beneath his thick eyebrows and the distance between the short nose and the thin lips is too long…. All this reminds me of some one. But of whom? And what is this curious habit I have of being reminded of some one? Probably a saint?

For a moment the cardinal was lost in thought and suddenly I recalled: Yes, this is simply a shaven *monkey*! This must be its sad, boundless pensiveness, *its* evil gleam within the narrow pupil!

But in a moment the Cardinal laughed, jested and gesticulated like a Neapolitan lazzarone—he was no longer telling me the history of the palace. He was playing, he was interpreting it in facial expression and dramatic monologue! He has short fingers, not at all like those of a monkey, and when he gesticulates he rather resembles a penguin while his voice reminds me of a talking parrot—Who are you, anyhow?

No, a monkey! He is laughing again and I observe that he really does not know how to laugh. It is as if he had learned the human art of laughter but yesterday. He likes it but experiences considerable difficulty in extracting it from his throat. The sounds seem to choke him. It is impossible not to echo this strange contagious laughter. But it seems to break one's jaws and teeth and to petrify the muscles.

It was really remarkable. I was fascinated when Cardinal X. suddenly cut short his lecture on the Villa Orsini by a fit of groaning laughter which left him calm and silent. His thin fingers played with his rosary, he remained quiet and gazed at me with a mien of deepest reverence and gentle love: something akin to tears glistened in his dark eyes. I had made an impression upon him. He loved me!

What was I to do? I gazed into his square, ape-like face. Kindliness turned to love, love into passion, and still we maintained the silence… another moment and I would have stifled him in my embrace!

"Well, here you are in Rome, Mr. Wondergood," sweetly sang the old monkey, without altering his loving gaze.

"Here I am in Rome," I agreed obediently, continuing to gaze upon him with the same sinful passion.

"And do you know, Mr. Wondergood, why I came here, i.e., in addition, of course, to the pleasure I anticipated in making your acquaintance?"

I thought and with my gaze unchanged, replied:

"For money, Your Eminence?"

The Cardinal shook, as though flapping his wings, laughed, and slapped his knee—and again lost himself in loving contemplation of my nose. This dumb reverence, to which I replied with redoubled zest, began to wield a peculiar influence upon me. I purposely tell you all this in detail in order that you may understand my wish at that moment: to begin cavorting about, to sing like a cock, to tell my best Arkansas anecdote, or simply to invite His Eminence to remove his regalia and play a game of poker!

"Your Eminence…."

"I love Americans, Mr. Wondergood."

"Your Eminence! In Arkansas they tell a story...."

"Ah, I see, you want to get down to business? I understand your impatience. Money matters should never be postponed. Is that not so?"

"It depends entirely upon one's concern in these matters, Your Eminence."

The square face of the Cardinal grew serious, and in his eyes there gleamed for a moment a ray of loving reproach:

"I hope you are not vexed at my long dissertation, Mr. Wondergood. I love so much the history of our great city that I could not forego the pleasure...the things you see before you are not Rome. There is no Rome, Mr. Wondergood. Once upon a time it was the Eternal City, but to-day it is simply a large city and the greater it grows the further it is from eternity. Where is that great Spirit which once illumined it?"

I shall not narrate to you all the prattle of this purple parrot, his gently-cannibal look, his grimaces and his laughter. All that the old shaven monkey told me when it finally grew weary was:

"Your misfortune is that you love your fellow beings too much...."

"Love your neighbor...."

"Well, let neighbors love each other. Go on teaching that but why do *you* want to do it? When one loves too well one is blind to the shortcomings of the beloved and still worse: one elevates these faults to virtues. How can you reform people and make them happy without realizing their shortcomings or by ignoring their vices? When one loves, one pities and pity is the death of power. You see, I am quite frank with you, Mr. Wondergood, and I repeat: love is weakness. Love will get the money out of your pocket and will squander it...on rouge! Leave love to the lower classes. Let them love each other. Demand it of them, but you, you have risen to greater heights, gifted with such power!..."

"But what can I do, Your Eminence? I am at a loss to understand it all. From my childhood on, especially in church, I have had it drummed into me that one must love his neighbor, and I believed it. And so...."

The Cardinal grew pensive. Like laughter, pensiveness was becoming to him and rendered his square face immovable, filling it with dignity and lonely grief. Leaning forward with his lips compressed and supporting his chin upon his hand, he fixed his sharp, sleepy eyes upon me. There was much sorrow in them. He seemed to be waiting for the conclusion of my remark, and not having patience to do so, sighed and blinked.

"Childhood, yes"...he mumbled, still blinking sorrowfully. "Children, yes. But you are no longer a child. Forget this lesson. You must acquire the heavenly gift of forgetfulness, you know."

He gnashed his white teeth and significantly scratched his nose with his thin finger, continuing seriously:

"But it's all the same, Mr. Wondergood. You, yourself cannot accomplish much.... Yes, yes! One must *know* people to make them happy. Isn't that your noble aim? But the Church alone *knows* people. She has been a mother and teacher for thousands of years. Her *experience* is the only one worth while, and, I may say, the only reliable one. As far as I know your career, Mr. Wondergood, you are an experienced cattle man. And you know, of course, what *experience* means even in the matter of handling such simple creatures as...."

"As swine...."

He was startled—and suddenly began to bark, to cough, to whine: he was laughing again.

"Swine? that's fine, that's splendid, Mr. Wondergood, but do not forget that one finds the devil, too, in swine!"

Ceasing his laughter he proceeded:

"In teaching others, we learn ourselves. I do not contend that all the methods of education and training employed by the Church were equally successful. No, we often made mistakes, but every one of our mistakes served to improve our methods...we are approaching perfection, Mr. Wondergood, we are approaching perfection!"

I hinted at the rapid growth of rationalism which, it seemed to me, threatened to destroy the "perfection" of the Church, but Cardinal X. again flapped his wings and almost screeched with laughter.

"Rationalism! You are a most talented humorist, Mr. Wondergood! Tell me, was not the celebrated Mark Twain a countryman of yours? Yes, yes! Rationalism! Just think a moment. From what root is this word derived and what does it mean—*ratio*? *An nescis, mi filis quantilla sapientia rigitur orbis*? Ah, my dear Wondergood! To speak of ratio on this earth is more out of place than it would be to speak of a rope in the home of a man who has just been hanged!"

I watched the old monkey enjoying himself and I enjoyed myself too. I studied this mixture of a monkey, parrot, penguin, fox, wolf—and what not? And it was really funny: I love merry suicides. For a long time we continued our fun at the expense of *ratio* until His Eminence calmed himself and assumed the tone of a teacher:

"As anti-Semitism is the Socialism of fools...."

"And are you familiar...?"

"I told you we are approaching perfection!... So is rationalism the wisdom of fools. The wise man goes further. The ratio constitutes the holiday dress of a fool. It is the coat he dons in the presence of others, but he really lives, sleeps, works, loves and dies without any ratio at all. Do you fear death, Mr. Wondergood?"

I did not feel like replying and remained silent.

"You need not feel ashamed, Mr. Wondergood: one should fear death. As long as there is *death*...."

The features of the monkey's face suddenly contracted and in his eyes there appeared horror and wrath: as if some one had seized him by the back of his neck and thrust him into the darkness and terror of a primeval forest. He *feared* death and his terror was dark, evil and boundless. I needed no words of explanation and no other evidence: One look upon this distorted, befogged and confused *human* face was sufficient to compel reverence for the Great Irrational! And how weak is *their* steadiness: My Wondergood also grew pale and cringed...ah, the rogue! He was *now* seeking protection and help from Me!

"Will you have some wine, Your Eminence?"

But His Eminence was himself again. He curved his thin lips into a smile and shook his head in the negative. And suddenly he broke out again with surprising fury:

"And as long as there is death, the Church is unshakable! Let all of you who seek to undermine her, tear her, and blow her up—you cannot conquer her. And even if you should succeed in destroying her, the first to perish beneath her ruins would be yourselves. Who will then defend you against death? Who will give you sweet faith in immortality, in eternal life, in everlasting bliss?... Believe me, Mr. Wondergood, the world is not seeking your ratio. It is all a misunderstanding!"

"But what does it seek, Your Eminence?"

"What does it want? *Mundus vult decipi*...you know our Latin? the world wants to be fooled!"

And the old monkey again grew merry, begun to wink, to beam with satisfaction, slapped his knee and burst into laughter. I also laughed. The rascal was so funny!

"And is it you," said I, "who wants to fool it?"

The Cardinal again grew serious and replied sadly:

"The Holy See needs funds, Mr. Wondergood. The world, while it has not grown rational, has become weaker in its faith and it is somewhat difficult to manage it."

He signed and continued:

"You are not a Socialist, Mr. Wondergood? Ah, do not be ashamed. We are all Socialists now. We are all on the side of the hungry: the more satisfied they will be, the more they will fear *death*. You understand?"

He flung out his arms and drew them in again, like a net filled with fish and said:

"We are fishermen, Mr. Wondergood, humble fishermen!... And tell me: do you regard the desire for *liberty* as a virtue or a vice?"

"The entire civilized world regards the desire for liberty as a virtue," I replied angrily.

"I expected no other reply from a citizen of the United States. But don't you personally believe that he who will give man limitless *freedom* will also bring him *death*? *Death* alone releases all earthly ties. And don't you regard the words 'freedom' and 'death' as synonymous?"

"I speak of political liberty."

"Of political liberty? Oh, we have no objection to that. You can have as much as you please of that! Of course, provided men themselves ask for it. Are you sure they really want it? If they do, please help yourself! It is all nonsense and calumny to say that the Holy See is in favor of reaction.... I had the honor to be present on the balcony of the Vatican when His Holiness blessed the first French aëroplane that appeared over Rome, and the next Pope, I am sure, will gladly bless the barricades. The time of Galileo has passed, Mr. Wondergood, and we all know now that the earth does move!"

He drew a circle in the air with his finger, indicating the revolution of the earth.

I said:

"You must permit me to think over your proposal, Your Eminence."

Cardinal X. jumped up from his chair and gently touched my shoulder with two of his aristocratic fingers:

"Oh, I am not hurrying you, my good Mr. Wondergood. It was you who were hurrying me. I am even convinced that you will at first refuse me, but when, after some little experience, you will have realized the real *needs* of man.... I, too, love man, Mr. Wondergood, to be sure, not so passionately and...."

He departed with the same grimaces, bearing himself with dignity and dispensing blessings all about him. I saw him again through the window at the entrance of the palace, while the coachman was bringing up the carriage: he was speaking into the ear of one of his abbés, whose face resembled a black plate. The Cardinal's countenance no longer reminded me of a monkey: it was rather the face of a shaven, hungry, tired lion. This able actor needed no dressing room for his make-up! Behind him stood a tall lackey, all dressed in black, reminding one of an English baronet. Whenever His Eminence turned about in his direction, he would respectfully lift his faded silk hat.

***

Following the departure of His Eminence I was surrounded by a merry group of friends, with whom I had filled the spare rooms of my palace for the purpose of alleviating my loneliness and ennui. Toppi looked proud and happy: he was so satiated with blessings that he fairly bulged. The artists, decorators and others—whatever you call them—were greatly impressed by the Cardinal's visit, and spoke with much glee of the remarkable expression of his face and the grandeur of his manner! The Pope himself…. But when I remarked with the naïveté of a Redskin that he reminded me of a monkey, the shrewd canailes burst into loud laughter and one of them immediately sketched a portrait of Cardinal X.—in a cage. I am not a moralist to judge other people for their petty sins: they will get what is due them on their Judgment Day—and I was much pleased by the cleverness of the laughing beasts. They do not appear to have much faith in *love* for one's *fellow beings* and if I should rummage about among their drawings, I would probably find a pretty good sketch of the ass Wondergood. I like that. I find relief in communion with my little, pleasant sinners, from the babbling of the great and disagreeable saints…whose hands are covered with blood.

Then Toppi asked me: "And how much does he want?"

"He wants all!"

Toppi said with determination:

"Don't you give him all. He promised to make me a prelate, but, all the same, don't you give him all. One should save his money."

Every day I have unpleasant experiences with Toppi: people are constantly foisting counterfeit coin on him. When they first gave him some, he was greatly perturbed and was impressed with what I said to him.

"You really astonish me, Toppi," I said, "it is ridiculous for an old devil like you to accept counterfeit money from human beings, and allow yourself to be fooled. You ought to be ashamed of yourself, Toppi. I fear you will make a beggar of me."

Now, however, Toppi, entangled in the mesh of the counterfeit and the genuine, seeks to preserve both the one and the other: he is quite clever in money matters and the Cardinal tried in vain to bribe him. Toppi—a prelate!…

But the shaven monkey does really want my three billions. Apparently the belly of the Holy See is rumbling with hunger. I gazed long at the well executed caricature of the Cardinal and the longer I gazed, the less I liked it: no, there was something missing. The artist had sensed the ridiculous pretty well, but I do not see that fire of spite and malice which is in constant play beneath the gray ashes of terror. The bestial and the human is here, but it is not molded into that *extraordinary* mask which, now that a long distance separates me from the Cardinal and I no longer hear his heavy laughter, is beginning to exercise a most disagreeable influence over me. Or is it because the extraordinary is inexpressible through pencil?

In reality he is a cheap rascal, no better than a plain pickpocket, and told me nothing new: he is human enough and wise enough to cultivate that contemptuous laughter of his at the expense of the rational. But he revealed *himself* to me and do not take offense at my American rudeness, dear reader: somewhere behind his broad shoulders, cringing with terror, there gleamed also your dear countenance. It was like a dream, you understand: it was as if some one were strangling you, and you, in stifled voice, cried to heaven: Murder! Police! Ah, you do not know that *third*, which is neither life nor death, and I know *who* it was that was strangling you with his bony fingers!

But do I know? Oh, laugh at him who is laughing at you, comrade. I fear your turn is coming to have some fun at my expense. Do I know? I came to you from the innermost depths, merry and serene, blessed in the consciousness of my Immortality.... And I am already hesitating. I am already trembling before this shaven monkey's face which dares to express its own low horror in such audaciously grand style: Ah, I have not even sold my Immortality: I have simply crushed it in my sleep, as does a foolish mother her newborn babe. It has simply faded beneath your sun and rains. It has become a transparent cloth without design, unfit to cover the nakedness of a respectable gentleman! This reeking Wondergood swamp in which I am submerged to my eyes, envelops me with mire, befogs my consciousness and stifles me with the unbearable odors of decay. When do you usually begin to decay, my friend: on the second, the third day or does it depend upon the climate? I am already in the process of decay, and I am nauseated by the odor of my entrails. Or are you so used to the work of the *worms* that you take it for the elevation of thought and inspiration?

My God, I forgot that I may have some fair readers, too! I most humbly beg your pardon, worthy folk, for this uncalled for discussion of odors. I am a most unpleasant conversationalist, milady, and as a perfumer I am worse...no, still worse: I am a disgusting mixture of Satan and an American bear, and I know not how to appreciate your good taste....

No, I am still Satan! I still know that I am immortal and when my will shall command me I will strangle myself with my own bony fingers. But if I *should forget*?

Then I shall distribute my wealth among the poor and with you, my friend, shall crawl up to the old shaven monkey. I shall cling with my American face to his soft slipper, emitting blessings. I shall weep. I shall rave with horror: "Save me from Death!" And the old monkey, brushing the hair from his face, reclining comfortably, gleaming with a holy light, illuminating all about it—and itself trembling with fear and horror—will hastily continue to fool the world, the world which so loves to be fooled!

But I am jesting. I wish to be serious now. I like Cardinal X. and I shall permit him to begild himself with my gold. I am weary. I must sleep. My bed and Wondergood await me. I shall extinguish the light and in the darkness I shall listen for a moment to the clicking of the counting machine within my breast. And then will come the great pianist, a drunken genius, and begin drumming upon the black keys of my brain. He knows everything and has forgotten everything, this ingenious drunkard, and confuses the most inspiring landscapes with a swamp.

That is—a dream.

II

February 22. Rome, Villa Orsini.

agnus was not at home. I was received by Maria.

A glorious peace has suddenly descended upon me. In wondrous calm I breathe at this moment. Like a schooner, its sails lowered, I doze in the midday heat of the slumbering ocean. Not a stir. Not a ripple. I fear to move or to open wide my eyes, dazzled by the rays of the sun. I breathe silently, and I would not rouse the slightest wave upon the boundless smoothness of the sea. And quietly I lay down my pen.

February 23. Villa Orsini.

Thomas Magnus was not at home and, to my great surprise, I was received by Maria.

I do not suppose you would be interested in how I greeted her and what I mumbled in the first few moments of our meeting. I can only say that I mumbled and that I felt a strong impulse to laugh. I could not lift my eyes to gaze upon Maria until my thoughts cast off their soiled garb and donned clean attire. As you see, I did not lose consciousness altogether! But in vain did I take these precautions: *that* torture did not follow. Maria's gaze was clear and simple and it contained neither searching, penetrating fire nor fatal forgiveness. It was calm and clear, like the sky of the Campagna and—I do not know how it happened—it penetrated my entire being.

She met me in the garden. We sat down by the gate, from which vantage point we had a good view of the Campagna. When you gaze at the Campagna you cannot prattle nonsense. No, it was she who gazed at the Campagna and I gazed into her eyes—clear to the seventh sky, where you end the count of your heavens. We were silent or—if you regard the following as conversation—we spoke:

"Are those mountains?"

"Yes, those are the mountains of Albania. And there—is Tivoli."

She picked out little white houses in the distance and pointed them out to me and I felt a peculiar calm and joy in Maria's gaze. The suspicious resemblance of Maria to the Madonna no longer troubled me: how can I possibly be troubled by the fact that you resemble *yourself*? And came a moment when a great peace of mind descended upon *me*. I have no words of comparison whereby to reveal to you that great and bright calm…. I am forever conjuring up before me that accursed schooner with its lowered sails, on which I never really sailed, for I am afraid of seasickness! Or is it because on this night of my loneliness, my road is being illuminated by the *Star of the Seas*? Well, yes, I was a schooner, if you so desire it, and if this is not agreeable to you I was *All*. Besides I was *Nothing*. You see what nonsense emerges out of all this talk when Wondergood begins to seek words and comparisons.

I was so calm that I even soon began to gaze into Maria's eyes: I simply *believed* them. This is deeper than mere gazing. When necessary I shall find those eyes again. In the meantime I shall remain a schooner with sails lowered. I shall be *All* and I shall be *Nothing*. Only once did a slight breeze stir my sails, but only for a moment: that was when Maria pointed out the Tiberian road to me, cutting the green hills like a white thread, and asked whether I had ever traversed it before.

"Yes, occasionally, Signorina."

"I often gaze upon this road and think that it must be extremely pleasant to traverse it by automobile."

"Have you a swift car, Signor?"

"Oh, yes, Signorina, very swift! But those," I continued in gentle reproach, "who are themselves limitless distances and endlessness are in no need of any movement."

Maria and an automobile! A winged angel entering a trolley car for the sake of speed! A swallow riding on a turtle! An arrow on the humpy back of a hod carrier! Ah, all comparisons lie: why speak of swallows and arrows, why speak of any movement for Maria, who embraces all distances! But it is only now that I thought of the trolley and the turtle. At that time I felt so calm and peaceful, I was deep in such bliss that I could think of nothing except that countenance of eternity and undying light!

A great calm came upon Me on that day and nothing could disturb my endless bliss. It was not long before Thomas Magnus returned, and a flying fish, gleaming for a moment above the ocean, could no more disturb its blue smoothness than did Magnus disturb me. I *received* him into my heart. I swallowed him calmly and felt no heavier burden in my stomach than a whale does after swallowing a herring. It was gratifying to find Magnus hospitable and merry. He pressed my hand and his eyes were bright and kind. Even his face seemed less pale and not as weary as usual.

I was invited to breakfast…lest it worry you, let me say right now that I remained until late in the evening. When Maria had retired I told Magnus of the visit of Cardinal X. His merry face darkened slightly and in his eyes appeared his former hostile flame.

"Cardinal X.? He *came* to see you?"

I narrated to him in detail my conversation with "the shaven monkey," and remarked that he had impressed me as a scoundrel of no small caliber. Magnus frowned and said sternly:

"You laugh in vain, Mr. Wondergood. I have long known Cardinal X. and…I have been keeping a close eye on him. He is evil, cruel and dangerous. Despite his ridiculous exterior, he is as cunning, merciless and revengeful as Satan!"

And you, too, Magnus! Like Satan! This blue-faced, shaven orang-outang, this caressing gorilla, this monkey cavorting before a looking-glass! But I have exhausted my capacity for insult. Magnus' remark fell like a stone to the bottom of my bliss. I listened further:

"His flirting with the Socialists, his jokes at the expense of Galileo are all lies. Just as the enemies of Cromwell hanged him after his death, so would Cardinal X. burn the bones of Galileo with immense satisfaction: to this day he regards the movement of the earth as a personal affront. It is an old school, Mr. Wondergood; he will stop at nothing to overcome obstacles, be it poison or murder, which he will take care to attribute to the misfortune of accident. You smile but I cannot discuss the Vatican smilingly, not so long as it contains such…and it will always produce some one like Cardinal X. Look out, Mr. Wondergood: You have landed within the sphere of his vision and interests, and, let me assure you, that scores of eyes are now watching you…perhaps me, too. Be on your guard, my friend!"

Magnus was quite excited. Fervently I shook his hand:

"Ah, Magnus!… But when will you agree to help me?"

"But you know that I do not like human beings. It is *you* who loves them Mr. Wondergood, not I."

A gleam of irony appeared in his eyes.

"The Cardinal says that it is not at all necessary to love people in order to be happy…. The contrary, he says!"

"And who told you that I want to make people happy? Again, it is *you* who wants to do that, not I. Hand over your billions to Cardinal X. His recipe for happiness is not worse than other patent medicines. To be sure, his recipe has one disadvantage: while dispensing *happiness* it destroys *people*…but is that important? You are too much of a business man, Mr. Wondergood, and I see that you are not sufficiently familiar with the world of our inventors of the Best Means for the Happiness of Mankind: These means are more numerous than the so-called best tonics for the growth of hair. I myself was a dreamer at one time and invented one or two in my youth…but I was short on chemistry and badly singed my hair in an explosion. I am very glad I did not come across your billions in *those* days. I am joking, Mr. Wondergood, but if you wish to be serious, here is my answer: keep on growing and multiplying your hogs, make four of your three billions, continue selling your conserves, provided they are not too rotten, and cease worrying about the happiness of Mankind. As long as the world likes good ham it will not deny you its love and admiration!"

"And how about those who have no means to buy ham?"

"What do you care about them? It is their belly—pardon me for the expression—that is rumbling with hunger, not yours. I congratulate you upon your new home: I know the Villa Orsini very well. It is a magnificent relic of Old Rome."

I balked at the prospect of another lecture on my palace! Yes, Magnus had again shoved me aside. He did it brusquely and roughly. But his voice lacked sternness and he gazed at me softly and kindly. Well, what of it? To the devil with humanity, its happiness and its ham! I shall try later to bore an entrance into Magnus' brain. In the meantime leave me alone with my great peace and…Maria. Boundless peace and…Satan!—isn't that a splendid touch in my play? And what kind of a liar is he who can fool only others? To lie to oneself and believe it—that is an art!

After breakfast all *three* of us walked over the downy hills and slopes of the Campagna. It was still early Spring and only little white flowers gently brightened the young, green earth. A soft breeze diffused the scents of the season, while little houses gleamed in distant Albano. Maria walked in front of us, stopping now and then and casting her heavenly eyes upon everything they could envisage. When I return to Rome I shall order my brush-pusher to paint Madonna thus: On a carpet of soft green and little white flowers. Magnus was so frank and merry that I again drew his attention to Maria's resemblance to the Madonna and told him of the miserable brush-pushers in search of a model. He laughed, agreed with me in my opinion of the aforementioned resemblance, and grew wistful.

"It is a *fatal* resemblance, Mr. Wondergood. You remember that heavy moment when I spoke to you of *blood*? Already there is blood at the feet of Maria…the blood of one noble youth whose memory Maria and I cherish. There are fatal faces, there are fatal *resemblances* which confuse our souls and lead to the abyss of self destruction. I am the father of Maria, and yet I myself hardly dare to touch her brow with my lips. What insurmountable barriers does love raise for itself when it dares to lift its eyes upon Maria?"

This was the only moment of that happy day when my ocean became overcast with heavy clouds, as tangled as the beard of "Mad King Lear," while a wild wind shook the sails of my schooner. But I lifted my eyes to Maria, I met her gaze. It was bright and calm, like the sky above us—and the wild wind disappeared without trace, bearing away with it fragments of the darkness. I do not know whether you understand these sea comparisons, which I consider quite inadequate. Let me explain: I again grew quite calm. What is that noble Roman youth to me, who himself unable to find *comparisons* was hurled over the head of his Pegasus? I am a white-winged schooner and beneath me is an entire ocean, and was it not written of Her: the *Incomparable*?

The day was long and quiet and I was charmed with the precision with which the sun rolled down from its height to the rim of the earth, with the measured pace with which the stars covered the heavens, the large stars first, then the little ones, until the whole sky sparkled and gleamed. Slowly grew the darkness. Then came the rosy moon, at first somewhat rusty, then brilliant, and swam majestically over the road made free and warm by the sun. But more than anything else did I and Magnus feel charmed when we sat in the half-darkened room and heard Maria: she played the harp and sang.

And listening to the strains of the harp I realized why man likes music produced by taut strings: I was myself a taut string and even when the finger no longer touched me, the sound continued to vibrate and died so slowly that I can still hear it in the depths of my soul. And suddenly I saw that the entire air was filled with taut and trembling strings: they extend from star to star, scatter themselves over the earth and penetrate my heart…like a network of telephone wires through a central station,— if you want more simple comparisons. And there was *something else* I understood when I heard *Maria's* voice….

No, you are simply an animal, Wondergood! When I recall your loud complaints against love and its songs, cursed with the curse of monotony—is that not your own expression?—I feel like sending you off to a barn. You are a dull and dirty animal and I am ashamed that for a whole hour I listened to your silly bellowing. You may hold words in contempt, you may curse your embraces, but do not touch Love, my friend: only through love has it been given to you to obtain a glimpse into Eternity! Away, my friend! Leave Satan to himself, he who in the very blackest depths of man has suddenly come upon new and unexpected flames. Away! You must not see the *joy* and *astonishment* of Satan!

The hour was late. The moon indicated midnight when I left Magnus and ordered the chauffeur to drive by way of the Numentinian road: I feared lest this great calm might slip away from me, and I wanted to overtake it in the depths of the Campagna. But the speed of the car broke the silence and I left my machine. It went to sleep at once beneath the light of the moon over its own shadow and looked like a huge, gray stone barring the road. For the last time its lights gleamed upon Me and it became transformed into something invisible. I was left alone with my shadow.

We walked along the white road, I and my shadow, stopping occasionally and then again resuming our march. I sat down on a stone along the road and the black shadow hid behind my back. And here a great quiet descended upon the earth, upon the world. Upon my chilled brow I felt the cool touch of the moon's kiss.

March 2. Rome, Villa Orsini.

I pass my days in deep solitude. My earthly existence is beginning to trouble me. With every hour I seem to *forget* what I have left behind the wall of *human* things. My *eyesight* is weakening. I can hardly see behind that wall. The shadows behind it scarcely move and I can no longer distinguish their outline. With every second my sense of *hearing* grows duller. I hear the quiet squeak of a mouse, fussing beneath the floor but I am deaf to the thunders rolling above my head. The silence of delusion envelops me and I desperately strain my ears to catch the voices of frankness. I left them behind that impenetrable wall. With each moment *Truth* flees from Me. In vain my words try to overtake it: they merely shoot by. In vain I seek to surround it in the tight embraces of my thoughts and rivet it with chains: the prison disappears like air and my embraces envelop nothing but emptiness. Only yesterday it seemed to me that I had caught my prey. I imprisoned it and fastened it to the wall with a heavy chain, but when I came to view it in the morning—I found nothing but a shackled skeleton. The rusty chains dangled loosely from its neck while the skull was nodding to me in brazen laughter.

You see, I am again seeking comparisons, only to have the *Truth* escape me! But what can I do when I have left all my weapons at *home* and must resort to your poor arsenal? Let God himself don this human form and He will immediately begin to speak to you in exquisite French or Yiddish and He will be unable to say *more* than it is possible to say in exquisite French or Yiddish. God! And I am only Satan, a modest, careless, human Devil!

Of course, it was careless of me. But when I looked upon *your human* life from *beyond*…no, wait: You and I have just been caught in a lie, old man! When I said from *Beyond* you understood at once it must have been very far away. Yes? You may have already determined, perhaps, the approximate number of miles. Have you not at your disposal a limitless number of zeros? Ah, it is not true. My *"Beyond"* is as close as your "*Here*," and is no further away than *this* very spot. You see what nonsense, what a lie you and I are pirouetting about! Cast away your meter and your scales and only listen as if behind your back there were no ticking of a clock and in your breast there were no counting machine. And so: when I looked upon your life from *Beyond* it appeared to Me a great and merry game of immortal fragments.

Do you know what a puppets' show is? When one doll breaks, its place is taken by another, but the play goes on. The music is not silenced, the auditors continue to applaud and it is all very interesting. Does the spectator concern himself about the fate of the fragments, thrust upon the scrap heap? He simply looks on in enjoyment. So it was with me, too. I heard the beat of the drums, and watched the antics of the clowns. And I so love immortal play that I felt like becoming an actor myself. Ah, I did not know then that it is not a *play* at all. And that the scrap heap was terrible when one becomes a puppet himself and that the broken fragments reeked with blood. You deceived me, my friend!

But you are astonished. You knit your brow in contempt and ask: Who is this Satan who does not *know* such *simple* things? You are accustomed to respect the Devil. You listen to the commonest dog as if he were speaking ex cathedra. You have surrendered to me your last dollar as if I were a professor of white and black magic and suddenly I reveal myself an ignoramus in the most elementary matters! I understand your disappointment. I myself have grown to respect mediums and cards. I am ashamed to confess that I cannot perform a single trick or kill a bed-bug by simply casting my eye upon it, but even with my finger. But what matters most to me is truth: Yes, I did not know your *simplest* things! Apparently the blame for this is for that *divide* which separates us. Just as you do not know *my* real Name and cannot pronounce a simple thing like that, so I did not know *yours*, my earthly shadow, and only now, in great ecstasy do I begin to grasp the wealth that is in you. Think of it: such a simple matter as counting I had to learn from Wondergood. I would not even be able to button my attire if it were not for the experienced and dexterous fingers of that fine chap Wondergood!

Now I am human, like you. The limited sensation of my being I regard as my *knowledge* and with respect I now touch my own nose, when necessity arises: it is not merely a nose—it is an axiom! I am now myself a struggling doll in a theater of marionettes. My porcelain head moves to the right and to the left. My hands move up and down. I am merry, I am gay. I am at play. I know everything…except: whose hand it is that pulls the string behind Me. And in the distance I can see the scrap heap from which protrude two little feet clad in ball slippers….

No, this is not the *play* of the *Immortal* that I sought. It no more resembles merriment than do the convulsions of an epileptic a good negro dance! Here any one is what he is and here every one seeks not to be what he is. And it is this endless process of fraud that I mistook for a merry theater: what a mistake, how silly it was of "almighty, immortal"…Satan! Here every one is dragging every one else to court: the living are dragging the dead, the dead—the living. The history of the former is the history of the latter. And God, too, is History! And this endless nonsense, this dirty stream of false witnesses, of perjurers, of false judges and false scoundrels I mistook for the *play* of immortals! Or have I landed in the *wrong* place? Tell Me, stranger: whither does *this* road lead? You are pale. Your trembling finger points in the direction of…ah, the scrap heap!

Yesterday, I questioned Toppi about his former life, the first time he donned the human form: I wanted to know how a doll feels when its head is cracking and the thread which moves it is severed. We lit our pipes and with steins of beer before us, like two good Germans, we ventured into the realm of philosophy. It developed, however, that this numbskull has *forgotten* everything and my questions only confused him.

"Is it possible that you have really forgotten everything, Toppi!"

"Wait till you die and you will learn all about it yourself. I do not like to think of it. What good is it?"

"Then it is not good?"

"And have you ever heard of any one praising it?"

"Quite true. No one has yet showered praises upon it."

"And no one will, I know!"

We sat silent.

"And do you remember, Toppi, whence you have come?"

"From Illinois,—the same place you come from."

"No, I am speaking of *something else*. Do you remember whence you came? Do you recollect your real Name?"

Toppi looked at me strangely, paled slightly and proceeded to clean his pipe. Then he arose and without lifting his eyes, said:

"I beg you not to speak to me *thus*, Mr. Wondergood. I am an honest citizen of the United States and I do not understand your insinuations."

But he remembers. Not in vain did he grow pale. He is seeking to forget and will forget soon enough! This double play of earth and heaven is too much for him and he has surrendered entirely to the earth! There will come a time when he will take me off to an insane asylum or betray me to Cardinal X. if I dare to speak to him of Satan.

"I respect you, Toppi. You are quite a man," I said and kissed his brow: I always kiss the brow of people I love.

Again I departed for the green Campagna desert: I follow the best models: when I am ill at ease I go into the desert. There I called for Satan and cursed his name but he would not answer me. I lay there long in the dust, pleading, when from somewhere in the depths of the desert I heard the muffled tread of feet, and a bright light helped Me to arise. And again I saw the Eden I had left behind, its green tents and unfading sunrise, its quiet lights upon the placid waters. And again I *heard* the silent murmurs of lips born of Immaculate Conception while toward my eyes I saw approaching Truth. And I stretched out my hands to Her and pleaded: Give me back my liberty!—

"*Maria!*"

Who called: Maria? Satan again departed, the lights upon the placid waters were extinguished and Truth, frightened, disappeared—and again I sit upon the earth wearing my human form and gazing dully upon the painted world. And on my knees rested my shackled hands.

"Maria!"

…It is painful for me to admit that all this is really an invention: the coming of Satan with his "light and ringing step," the gardens of Eden and my shackled hands. But I needed your attention and I could not get it without these gardens of Eden and these chains, the two extremes of your life. The gardens of Eden—how beautiful! Chains—how terrible! Moreover, all this talk is much more entertaining than merely squatting on a hill, cigar in one's *free* hand, thinking lazily and yawning while awaiting the arrival of the chauffeur. And as far as *Maria* is concerned, I brought her into the situation because from afar I could see the black cypress trees above the Magnus home. An involuntary association of ideas…you understand.

Can a man with such sight really see Satan? Can a person of such dull *ear* hear the so-called "murmurs" born of Immaculate Conception? Nonsense! And, please, I beg of you, call Me just Wondergood. Call me just Wondergood until the day when I crack my skull open with that plaything which opens the *most narrow* door into *limitless* space. Call me just Henry Wondergood, of Illinois: you will find that I will respond promptly and obligingly.

But if, some day, you should find my head crushed, examine carefully its *fragments*: there, in red ink will be engraved the proud name of Satan! Bend thy head, in reverence and bow to him—but do not do me the honor of accompanying my fragments to the scrap heap: one should never bow so respectfully to chains cast off!

March 9, 1914. Rome, Villa Orsini.

Last night I had an important conversation with Thomas Magnus. When Maria had retired I began as usual to prepare to return home but Magnus detained me.

"Why go, Mr. Wondergood? Stay here for the night. Stay here and listen to the barking of Mars!"

For several days dense clouds had been gathering over Rome and a heavy rain had been beating down upon its walls and ruins. This morning I read in a newspaper a very portentous weather bulletin: *cielo nuvolo il vento forte e mare molto agitato.* Toward evening the threat turned into a storm and the enraged sea hurled across a range of ninety miles its moist odors upon the walls of Rome. And the real Roman sea, the billowy Campagna, sang forth with all the voices of the tempest, like the ocean, and at moments it seemed that its immovable hills, its ancient waves, long evaporated by the sun, had once more come to life and moved forward upon the city walls. Mad Mars, this creator of terror and tempest, flew like an arrow across its wide spaces, crushed the head of every blade of grass to the ground, sighed and panted and hurled heavy gusts of wind into the whining cypress trees. Occasionally he would seize and hurl the nearest objects he could lay his hands upon: the brick roofs of the houses shook beneath his blows and their stone walls roared as if inside the very stones the imprisoned wind was gasping and seeking an escape.

We listened to the storm all evening. Maria was calm but Magnus was visibly nervous, constantly rubbed his white hands and listened intently to the antics of the wind: to its murderous whistle, its roar and its signs, its laughter and its groans…the wild-haired artist was cunning enough to be slayer and victim, to strangle and to plead for mercy at one and the same time! If Magnus had the moving ears of an animal, they would have remained immovable. His thin nose trembled, his dim eyes grew dark, as if they reflected the shadows of the clouds, his thin lips were twisted into a quick and strange smile. I, too, was quite excited: it was the first time since I became human I had heard such a storm and it raised in me a white terror: almost with the horror of a child I avoided the windows, beyond which lay the night. Why does it not come here, I thought: can the window pane possibly keep it out if it should wish to break through?…

Some one knocked at the iron gates several times, the gates at which I and Toppi once knocked for admission.

"That is my chauffeur, who has come to fetch me," said I: "we must admit him."

Magnus glanced at me from the corner of his eye and remarked sadly:

"There is no road on that side of the house. There is nothing but field there. That is mad Mars who is begging for admittance."

And as if he had actually heard his words, Mars broke out into laughter and disappeared whistling. But the knocking was soon resumed. It seemed as if some one were tearing off the iron gates and several voices, shouting and interrupting each other, were anxiously speaking; an infant was heard weeping.

"Those must be people who have lost their way…you hear—an infant! We must open the gates."

"Well, we'll see," said Magnus angrily.

"I will go with you, Magnus."

"Sit still, Wondergood. This friend of mine, here, is quite enough.…" He quickly drew *that* revolver from the table drawer and with a peculiar expression of love and even gentleness he grasped it in his broad hand and carefully hid it in his pocket. He walked out and we could hear the cry that met him at the gate.

On that evening I somehow avoided Maria's eyes and I felt quite ill at ease when we were left alone. And suddenly I felt like sinking to the floor, and kneeling before her so that her dress might touch my face: I felt as if I had hair on my back, that sparks would at any moment begin to fly if some one were to touch it and that this would relieve me. Thus, in my mind, I moved closer and closer to Her, when Magnus returned and silently put the revolver back into the drawer. The voices at the door had ceased and the knocking, too.

"Who was that?"…asked Maria.

Magnus angrily shook off the drops of rain upon his coat.

"Crazy Mars. Who else did you expect?"

"But I thought I heard you speak to him?" I jested, trying to conceal the shiver produced by the cold brought in by Magnus.

"Yes, I told him it was not polite—to drag about with him such suspicious company. He excused himself and said he would come no more," Magnus laughed and added: "I am convinced that all the murderers of Rome and the Campagna are to-night threatening to ambush people and hugging their stilettos as if they were their sweethearts.…"

Again came a muffled and timid knock.

"Again!" cried Magnus, angrily, as if Mad Mars had really promised to knock no more. But the knock was followed by the ring of a bell: it was my chauffeur. Maria retired, while I, as I have already said, had been invited by Magnus to remain overnight, to which I agreed, after some hesitation: I was not at all taken by Magnus and his revolver, and still less was I attracted by the silly darkness.

The kind host himself went out to dismiss the chauffeur. Through the window I could see the bright lights of the lanterns of the machine and for a moment I yearned to return home to my pleasant sinners, who were probably imbibing their wine at that moment in expectation of my return.... Ah, I have long since abandoned philanthropy and am now leading the life of a drunkard and a gambler. And again, as on that first night, the quiet little white house, this *soul* of Maria, looked terrible and suspicious: this revolver, these stains of *blood* upon the white hands... and, maybe there are more stains like these here.

But it was too late to change my mind. The machine had gone and Magnus, by the light, had not a *blue*, but a very black and beautiful beard and his eyes were smiling pleasantly. In his broad hand he carried not a weapon, but two bottles of wine, and from afar he shouted merrily:

"On a night like this there is but one thing to do, to drink wine. Even Mars, when I spoke to him, looked drunk to me...the rogue! Your glass, Mr. Wondergood!"

But when the glasses had been filled, this merry drunkard hardly touched the wine and sitting deep in his chair asked me to drink and to talk. Without particular enthusiasm, listening to the noise of the wind and thinking about the length of the night before us, I told Magnus of the new and insistent visits of Cardinal X. It seemed to me that the Cardinal had actually put spies on my trail and what is more strange: he has managed to gain quite an influence over the unbribable Toppi. Toppi is still the same devoted friend of mine but he seems to have grown sad, goes to confessional every day and is trying to persuade me to accept Catholicism.

Magnus listened calmly to my story and with still greater reluctance I told him of the many unsuccessful efforts to open my purse: of the endless petitions, badly written, in which the truth appears to be falsehood because of the boresome monotony of tears, bows and naïve flattery; of crazy inventors, of all sorts of people with hasty projects, gentlemen who seek to utilize as quickly as possible their temporary absence from jail—of all this hungry mass of humanity aroused by the smell of *weakly* protected billions. My secretaries—there are six of them now—hardly manage to handle all this mess of tears on paper, and the madly babbling fools who fill the doors of my palace.

"I fear that I will have to build me an underground exit: they are watching me even at nights. They are aiming at me with picks and shovels, as if they were in the Klondike. The nonsense published by these accursed newspapers about the billions I am ready to give away to every fool displaying a wound in his leg, or an empty pocket, has driven them out of their senses. I believe that some night they will divide me into portions and eat me. They are organizing regular pilgrimages to my palace and come with huge bags. My ladies, who regard me as their property, have found for me a little Dante Inferno, where we take daily walks in company with the society that storms my place. Yesterday we examined an old witch whose entire worth consists in the fact that she has outlived her husband, her children and her grandchildren, and is now in need of snuff. And some angry old man refused to be consoled and even would not take any money until all of us had smelled the old putrid wound in his foot. It was indeed a horrible odor. This cross old fellow is the pride of my ladies, and like all favorites, he is capricious, and temperamental. And…are you tired of listening to me, Magnus. I could tell you of a whole flock of ragged fathers, hungry children, green and rotten like certain kinds of cheese, of noble geniuses who despise me like a negro, of clever drunkards with merry, red noses…. My ladies are not very keen on drunkards, but I love them better than any other kind of goods. And how do you feel about it, Signor Magnus?"

Magnus was silent. I too was tired of talking. Mad Mars alone continued his antics: he was now ensconced upon the roof, trying to bite a hole in the center, and crushing the tiles as he would a lump of sugar. Magnus broke the silence:

"The newspapers seem to have little to say about you recently. What is the matter?"

"I pay the interviewers not to write anything. At first I drove them away but they began interviewing my horses and now I pay them for their silence by the line. Have you a customer for my villa, Magnus? I shall sell it together with the artists and the rest of its paraphernalia."

We again grew silent and paced up and down the room: Magnus rose first and then sat down. I followed and sat down too. In addition, I drank two more glasses of wine while Magnus drank none…. His nose is never red. Suddenly he said with determination:

"Do not drink any more wine, Wondergood."

"Oh, very well. I want no more wine. Is that all?"

Magnus continued to question me at long intervals. His voice was sharp and stern, while mine was…melodious, I would say.

"There has been a great change in you, Wondergood."

"Quite possible, thank you, Magnus."

"There used to be more life in you. Now you rarely jest. You have become very morose, Wondergood."

"Oh!"

"You have even grown thin and your brow is sallow. Is it true that you get drunk every night in the company of your…friends?"

"It seems so."

"…that you play cards, squander your gold, and that recently some one had been nearly murdered at your table?"

"I fear that is true. I recollect that one gentleman actually tried to pierce another gentleman with his fork. And how do you know all about that?"

He replied sternly and significantly:

"Toppi was here yesterday. He wanted to see…Maria but I myself received him. With all due respect to you, Wondergood, I must say that your secretary is unusually stupid."

I acquiesced coldly.

"You are quite right. You should have driven him out."

I must say for my part, that my last two glasses of wine evaporated from me at the mention of *Maria's* name, and our attempted conversation was marked by continued evaporation of the wine I drank, like perfume out of a bottle. I have always regarded wine as unreliable matter. We found ourselves again listening to the storm and I remarked:

"The wind seems to be growing more violent, Signor Magnus."

"Yes, the wind seems to be growing more violent, Mr. Wondergood. But you must admit that I warned you beforehand, Mr. Wondergood."

"Of what did you warn me beforehand, Signor Magnus?"

He seized his knees with his white hands and directed upon me the gaze of a snake charmer…. Ah, he did not know that I myself had extracted my poisoned teeth and was quite harmless, like a mummy in a museum! Finally, he realized that there was no use beating about the bush, and came straight to the point:

"I warned you in regard to *Maria*," he said slowly, with peculiar insinuation. "You remember that I did not desire your acquaintance and expressed it plainly enough? You have not forgotten *what* I told you about Maria, of her fatal influence upon the soul? But you were bold and insistent and I yielded. And now you ask us—me and my daughter—to view the highly exhilarating spectacle of a gentleman in the process of disintegration, one who asks nothing, who reproaches no one, but can find no solace until every one has smelled his wound…. I do not want to repeat your expression, Mr. Wondergood. It has a bad odor. Yes, sir, you have spoken quite frankly of your…neighbors and I am sincerely glad you have finally abandoned this cheap play at love and humanity…. You have so many other pastimes! I confess, however, that I am not at all overjoyed at your intention of presenting to *us* the *sediment* of a gentleman. It seems to me, sir, that you made a mistake in leaving America and your…canning business: dealing with people requires quite a different sort of ability."

He laughed! He was almost driving Me out, this little man, and I, who write my "I" in a super-capital, I listened to him humbly and meekly. It was divinely ridiculous! Here is another detail for those who love the ridiculous: before his tirade began my eyes and the cigar between my teeth were quite bravely and nonchalantly directed toward the ceiling, but they changed their attitude before he had finished…. To this very moment I feel the taste of that miserable dangling, extinguished cigar. I was choking with laughter…that is I did not yet know whether to choke with laughter or with wrath. Or, without choking at all, to ask him for an umbrella and leave. Ah, he was at *home*, he was on his *own* ground, this angry, black bearded man. He knew how to manage himself in this situation and he sang a *solo*, not a *duet*, like the inseparable Satan of Eternity and Wondergood of Illinois!

"Sir!" I said with dignity: "There seems to be a sad misunderstanding here. You see before you Satan in *human form*…you understand? He went out for an evening stroll and was lost in the forest…in the forest, sir, in the forest! Won't you be good enough, sir, to direct him to the nearest road to Eternity? Ah, Ah! Thank you. *So* I thought myself. Farewell!"

Of course, I really did not say that. I was *silent* and gave the floor to Wondergood. And this is what that respectable gentleman said, dropping his wet, dead cigar:

"The devil take it! You are quite right, Magnus. Thank you, old man. Yes, you warned me quite honestly, but I preferred to play a lone hand. Now I am a bankrupt and at your mercy. I shall have no objection if you should order the removal of the *sediment* of the gentleman."

I thought that without waiting for a stretcher, Magnus would simply throw the sediment out of the window, but his generosity proved quite surprising: he looked at Me with pity and even stretched out his hand.

"You are suffering very much, Mr. Wondergood?"—a question quite difficult to answer for the celebrated *duet*! I blinked and shrugged my shoulders. This appeared to satisfy Magnus and for a few moments we were both silent. I do not know of what Magnus was thinking. I thought of nothing: I simply examined with great interest, the walls, the ceiling, books, pictures—all the furnishings of this human habitation. I was particularly absorbed in the electric light upon which I fixed my attention: why does *it* burn and give light?

"I am waiting for your answer, Mr. Wondergood."

So he was really expecting me to reply? Very well.

"It's very simple, Magnus…you warned me, I admit. To-morrow Toppi will pack my trunks and I shall go back to America to resume my…business."

"And the Cardinal?"

"What Cardinal? Ah, yes!… Cardinal X. and my billions. I remember. But—don't gaze at me in such astonishment, Magnus. I am sick of it."

"What are you sick of, Mr. Wondergood?"

"*It*. Six secretaries. Brainless old women, snuff, and my Dante Inferno, where they take me for my walks. Don't look at me so sternly, Magnus. Probably one could have made better wine out of my billions, but I managed to produce only sour beer. Why did you refuse to help me? Of course, you hate human beings, I forgot."

"But you *love* them?"

"What shall I say, Magnus? No, I am rather indifferent to them. Don't look at me so…pityingly. By God, it isn't worth it! Yes, I am indifferent to them. There are, there were and there will be so many of them that it isn't really worth while…."

"So I am to conclude that you *lied*?"

"Look not at me but at my packed trunks. No, I did not lie, not entirely. You know, I wanted to do something interesting for the sake of amusement and so I let loose this…this emotion…."

"So it was only *play*?…"

I blinked again and shrugged my shoulders. I like this method of reply to complex questions. And *this* face of Signor Thomas Magnus appealed to me, too; his long, oval face recompensed me slightly for my theatrical failures and…Maria. I must add that by this time there was a fresh cigar in my mouth.

"You said that in your past there are some dark pages…. What's the trouble, Mr. Wondergood?"

"Oh! it was a slight exaggeration. Nothing in particular, Magnus. I beg your pardon for disturbing you needlessly, but at that time I thought I should have spoken thus for the sake of style…."

"Style?"

"Yes, and the laws of contrast. The present is always brighter with a dark past as a background…you understand? But I have already told you, Magnus, that my prank had little result. In the place I come from they have quite a mistaken conception of the pleasures of the game here. I shall have to disabuse them when I get back. For a moment I was taken in by the old monkey, but its method of fleecing people is rather ancient and too certain…like a counting house. I prefer an element of risk."

"Fleecing people?"

"Don't we despise them, Magnus? And if the game has failed, let us not at least deny ourselves the pleasure of speaking frankly. I am very glad. But I am tired of this prattle and, with your permission, I will take another glass of wine."

There was not even the resemblance of a smile on Thomas Magnus' face. I mention the smile for the sake of…style. We passed the next half hour in silence, broken only by the shrieks and yells of Mad Mars and the even pacing of Magnus. With his hands behind him and disregarding me entirely he paced the room with even step: eight steps forward, eight steps backward. Apparently he must have been in jail at one time and for quite a while: for he had the knack of the experienced prisoner of creating distances out of a few meters. I permitted myself to yawn slightly and thus drew the attention of my host back to myself. But Magnus kept quiet for another moment, until the *following words* rang out through the air and well nigh hurled me out of my seat:

"But *Maria* loves you. Of course, you do not know that?"

I arose.

"Yes, that is the truth: Maria loves you. I did not expect this misfortune. I failed to kill you, Mr. Wondergood. I should have done that at the very beginning and now I do not know what to do with you. What do you think about it?"

I stretched and…

***

…Maria loves *Me*!

I once witnessed in Philadelphia an unsuccessful electrocution of a prisoner. I saw at "La Scala" in Milan my colleague Mephisto *cringing* and hopping all over the stage when the supers moved upon him with their crosses—and my silent reply to Magnus was an artistic improvisation of both the first and the second trick: ah, at that moment I could think of nothing better to imitate! I swear by eternal salvation that never before had I been permeated by so many deadly currents, never did I drink such bitter wine, never was my soul seized with such uncontrollable *laughter*!

Now I no longer laugh or cringe, like a cheap actor. I am alone and only my own seriousness can hear and see Me. But in that moment of triumph I needed all my strength to control my laughter so that I might not deal ringing blows to the face of this stern and honest man hurling the Madonna into the embraces of…the Devil. Do you really think so? No? Or are you merely thinking of Wondergood, the American, with his goatee and wet cigar between his gold teeth! Hatred and contempt, love and anguish, wrath and laughter,—these filled to the brim the cup presented to Me…no, still worse, still more bitter, still more deadly! What do I care about the deceived Magnus or the stupidity of his eyes and brain? But how could the pure eyes of *Maria* have been deceived?

Or am I really such a clever Don Juan that I can turn the head of an innocent and trusting girl by a few simple, silent meetings? Madonna, where art Thou? Or, has she discovered a resemblance between myself and one of her saints, like Toppi's. But I do not carry with me a traveling prayer book! Madonna, where art Thou? Are thy lips stretching out to mine? Madonna, where art Thou? Or?…

And yet I cringed like an actor. I sought to stifle in respectful mumbling my hatred and my contempt when this new "*or*" suddenly filled me with new confusion and such love…ah, such love!

"*Or*," thought I, "has *Thy* immortality, Madonna, echoed the immortality of Satan and is it now stretching forth this gentle hand to it from the realms of Eternity? Thou, who art *divine*, hast thou recognized a friend in him who has become *human*? Thou, who art *above*, dost thou pity him who is *below*? Oh, Madonna, lay thy hand upon my dark head that I may recognize thee by thy touch!…"

But hear what further transpired that night.

***

"I know not why Maria has fallen in love with you. That is a secret of her soul, too much for my understanding. No, I do not know, but I bow to her will as to her frankness. What are my human eyes before her all-penetrating gaze, Mr. Wondergood!…"

(The latter, too, was saying the same thing.)

"A moment ago, in a fit of excitement," continued Magnus, "I said something about murder and death…. No, Mr. Wondergood, you may rest secure forever: the chosen one of Maria enjoys complete immunity as far as I am concerned. He is protected by more than the law—her pure love is his armor. Of course, I shall have to ask you to leave us at once. And I believe in your honest intention, Wondergood, to place the ocean between us…."

"But…."

Magnus moved forward towards me and shouted angrily:

"Not another word!… I cannot kill you but if you dare to mention the word 'marriage,' I!…"

He slowly dropped his uplifted hand, and continued calmly:

"I see that I will have to beg your pardon again for my fit of passion, but it is better than *falsehood*, examples of which we have had from you. Do not defend yourself, Wondergood. It is quite unnecessary. And of marriage let *me* speak: it will ring less insulting to Maria than it would from your lips. It is quite unthinkable. Remember that. I am a sober realist: I see nothing but mere coincidence in *that fatal* resemblance of Maria and I am not at all taken aback by the thought that my daughter, with all her unusual qualities, may some day become a wife and mother…. My categorical opposition to this marriage was simply another means of warning you. Yes, I am accustomed to look soberly upon things, Mr. Wondergood. It is not you who is destined to be Maria's life partner! You do not know me at all and now I am compelled to raise slightly the curtain behind which I am hiding these many years: my idleness is merely rest. I am not at all a peaceful villager or a book philosopher. I am a man of struggle. I am a warrior on the battlefield of life! And my Maria will be the gift only of a hero, if—if I should ever find a hero."

I said:

"You may rest assured, Signor Magnus, that I will not permit myself to utter a single word in regard to Signorina Maria. You know that I am not a hero. But I should think it permissible to ask of you: how am I to reconcile your present remarks with your former *contempt* for man? I recollect that you spoke seriously of gallows and prisons."

Magnus laughed loudly:

"And do you remember what you said about your *love* for man? Ah, my dear Wondergood: I would be a bad warrior and politician if my education did not embrace the art of lying a little. We were both playing, that's all!"

"You played better," I admitted quite gloomily.

"And you played very badly, my friend,—do not be offended. But what am I to do when there suddenly appears before me a gentleman all loaded with gold like...."

"Like an ass. Continue."

"And begins to reveal to me his love for humanity, while his confidence in his success is equal only to the quantity of the dollars in his pocket? The main fault of your play, Mr. Wondergood, is that you are too eager for success and seek immediate results. This makes the spectator cold and less credulous. To be sure, I really did not think you were merely acting—the worst play is better than sincere assininity—and I must again crave your pardon: you seemed to me just one of those foolish Yankees who really take their own bombastic and contemptible tirades seriously and...you understand?"

"Quite fully. I beg you to continue."

"Only one phrase of yours,—something about war and revolution purchasable with your billions—seemed to me to possess a modicum of interest, but the rest of the drivel proved that that, too, was a mere slip of the tongue, an accidental excerpt of some one else's text. Your newspaper triumphs, your flippancy in serious matters—remember Cardinal X!—your cheap philanthropy are of a quite different tone.... No, Mr. Wondergood, you are not fit for serious drama! And your prattling to-day, despite its cynicism, made a better impression than your flamboyant circus pathos. I say frankly: were it not for *Maria* I would gladly have had a good laugh at your expense, and, without the slightest compunction would have raised the farewell cup!"

"Just one correction, Magnus: I earnestly desired that you should take part...."

"In what? In your play? Yes, your play lacked the *creative factor* and you earnestly desired to saddle me with your poverty of spirit. Just as you hire your artists to paint and decorate your palaces so you wanted to hire my will and my imagination, my power and my love!"

"But your hatred for man...."

Up to this point Magnus had maintained his tone of irony and subtle ridicule: my remark, however, seemed to change him entirely. He grew pale, his white hands moved convulsively over his body as if they were searching for a weapon, and his face became threatening and even horrible. As if fearing the power of his own voice, he lowered it almost to a whisper; as if fearing that his words would break their leash and run off at a wild pace, he tried desperately to hold them in check and in order.

"Hatred? Be silent, sir. Or have you no conscience at all or any common sense? My contempt! My hatred! They were my reply, not to your theatrical *love*, but to your sincere and dead indifference. You were insulting *me* as a human being by your indifference: You were insulting life by your indifference. It was in your voice, it gleamed savagely out of your eyes, and more than once was I seized by terror...terror, sir!—when I pierced deeper the mysterious emptiness of your pupils. If your past has no dark pages, which, as you say, you merely added for the sake of style, then there is something worse than that in it: there are *white* pages in it. And I cannot read them!..."

"Oh, oh!"

"When I look at your eternal cigar, and see your self-satisfied but handsome and energetic face; when I view your unassuming manner, in which the simplicity of the grog shop is elevated to the heights of Puritanism, I fully understand your naïve game. But I need only meet the pupil of your eye...or its *white* rim and I am immediately hurled into a void, I am seized with alarm and I no longer see either your cigar or your gold teeth and I am ready to exclaim: who are you that you dare to bear yourself with such indifference?"

The situation was becoming interesting. *Madonna* loves Me and this creature is about ready to utter my Name at any moment! Is he the son of my Father? How could he unravel the great mystery of my boundless indifference: I tried so carefully to conceal it, even from you!

"Here! here!" shouted Magnus, in great excitement, "again there are two little tears in your eyes, as I have noticed before. They are a *lie*, Wondergood! There is no source of tears behind them. They have fallen from somewhere above, from the clouds, like dew. Rather laugh: behind your laughter I see merely a bad man, but behind your tears there are *white* pages, white pages!... or has Maria read them?"

Without taking his eyes off me, as if fearing that I might run away, Magnus paced the room, finally seating himself opposite Me. His face grew dim and his voice seemed tired, when he said:

"But it seems to me that I am exciting myself in vain...."

"Do not forget, Magnus, that to-day I myself spoke to you of indifference."

He waved his hand wearily and carelessly.

"Yes, you did speak. But there is something else involved here, Wondergood. There is nothing insulting in the indifference, but in the other...I sensed it immediately upon your appearance with your billions. I do not know whether you will understand what I mean, but I immediately felt like shouting of hatred and to demand gallows and blood. The gallows is a gloomy thing but the curious jostling about the gallows, Mr. Wondergood, are quite unbearable! I do not know what they think of our game here in the 'place' you come from, but we pay for it with our lives, and when there suddenly appears before us some curious gentleman in a top hat, cigar in mouth, one feels, you understand, like seizing him by the back of his neck and...he never stays to the end of the performance, anyway. Have you, too, Mr. Wondergood, dropped in on us for a brief visit?"

With what a long sigh I uttered the name of *Maria*!... And I no longer played, I no longer lied, when I replied to this gloomy man:

"Yes, I have dropped in on you for a brief visit, Signor Magnus. You have guessed right. For certain very valid reasons I can reveal nothing to you of the *white* pages of my life, the existence of which behind my leather binding you have likewise guessed. But on one of them was written: *death-departure*. That was not a top hat in the hands of the curious visitor, but a revolver...you understand: I look on as long as it is interesting and after that I make my bow and depart. Let me put it clearer and simpler, out of deference to your realism: in a few days, perhaps to-morrow, I depart for the other world.... No, that is not clear enough: in a few days or to-morrow I shall shoot myself, kill myself with a revolver. I at first planned to aim at my heart but have decided that the brain would be more reliable. I have planned all this long ago, at the very beginning... of my appearance before you, and was it not in this *readiness* of mine to depart that you have detected 'inhuman' indifference? Isn't it true that when one eye is directed upon the *other* world, it is hardly possible to maintain any particularly bright flame in the eye directed upon *this* world?... I refer to the kind of flame I see in your eyes. O! you have wonderful eyes, Signor Magnus."

Magnus remained silent for a few moments and then said:

"And Maria?"

"Permit me to reply. I prize Signorina Maria too highly not to regard her *love* for me as a fatal mistake."

"But you wanted that love?"

"It is very difficult for me to answer that question. At first, perhaps—when I indulged in dreams for a while—but the more I perceived this fatal resemblance...."

"That is mere resemblance," Magnus hastened to assure me: "But you mustn't be a child, Wondergood! Maria's soul is lofty and beautiful, but she is human, made of flesh and bone. She probably has her own little sins, too...."

"And how about my top hat, Magnus? How about my *free* departure? I need only buy a seat to gaze upon Maria and her fatal resemblance—admitting that it is only resemblance!—but how must I pay for *love*?"

Magnus said sternly:

"Only with your life."

"You see: only with my life! How, then, did you expect me to desire such love?"

"But you have miscalculated: she already loves you."

"Oh, if the Signorina Maria really loves me then my *death* can be no obstacle: however, I do not make myself clear. I wanted to say that my departure...no, I had better say nothing. In short, Signor Magnus: would you agree to have me place my billions at your disposal *now*?"

He looked at me quickly:

"Now?"

"Yes, now, when we are no longer playing: I at love and you at hatred. Now, when I am about to disappear entirely, taking with me the 'sediment' of a gentlemen? Let me make it quite clear: would you like to be my heir?"

Magnus frowned and looked at me in anger: apparently he took my words for ridicule. But I was calm and serious. It seemed to me that his large, white hands were trembling slightly. He turned away for a moment and then, whirling about quickly, he shouted loudly:

"No! Again you want.... No!"

He stamped his foot and cried once more: "No!" His hands were trembling. His breathing was heavy and irregular. There followed a long silence, the wailing of the tempest, the whistling and murmur of the wind. And again, great calm, great, dead, all embracing peace descended upon me. Everything was turned *within* Me. I still could hear the earthly demons of the storm, but *their* voices sounded far away and dull. I saw before me a *man* and he was strange and cold to me, like a stone statue. One after another there floated by me all the days of my human existence. There was the gleam of faces, the weak sound of voices and curious laughter. And then, again all was silent. I turned my gaze to the other side—and there I was met by dumbness. It was as if I were immured between two dumb, stone walls: behind one was *their* human life, which I had abandoned, and behind the other, in silence and in darkness, stretched forth the world of eternal and real being. Its silence was resounding, its darkness was gleaming, eternal, joyous life beat constantly like breakers, upon the hard rocks of the impenetrable wall. But deaf was my consciousness and silent my thought. From beneath the weak legs of Thought there came *Memory*—and it hung suspended in the void, immovable, paralyzed for the moment. *What* did I leave behind the wall of my Unconsciousness?

Thought made no reply. It was motionless, empty and silent. Two silences surrounded Me, two darknesses enveloped me. Two walls were burying me, and behind one, in the pale movement of shadows, passed their human life, while behind the other,—in silence and in darkness stretched forth the world of my real, eternal being. Whence shall I hear The Call? Whither can I take a step?

And at that moment I suddenly heard the voice of a man, strange and distant. It grew closer and closer, there was a gentle ring in it. It was Magnus speaking. With great effort and concentration, I tried to catch the words and this was what I heard:

"And wouldn't you rather continue living, Wondergood?"

March 18. Rome, Palazzo Orsini.

It is three days now that Magnus and Maria are living in my palazzo in Rome. It is empty and silent and really seems huge. Last night, worn by insomnia, I wandered about its halls and stairways, over rooms I had never seen before and their number astonished me. Maria's *soul* has expelled from it all that was frivolous and impure and only the saintly Toppi moves through its emptiness, like the pendulum of a church clock. Ah, how saintly he looks. If not for his broad back, the broad folds of his coat, and the odor of fur in his head, I myself would take him for one of the saints who have honored me with their acquaintance.

I rarely see my guests. I am turning my entire estate into cash and Magnus and Toppi and all the secretaries are busy with this work from morning to night; our telegraph is constantly buzzing. Magnus has little to say to me. He only talks business. Maria…it seems as if I were avoiding her. I can see her through my window walking in the garden, and this is quite enough for me, for her *soul* is here and every atom of the air is filled with her breath. And, as I have already remarked, I suffer with insomnia.

As you see, my friend, I have remained among the *living*, a dead hand could not possibly write even the dead words I am not setting down. Let us forget the past, as sweethearts would who have just settled their differences. Let us be friends, you and I. Give me your hand, my friend! I vow by eternal salvation that never again will I chase you hence or laugh at you: if I have lost the wisdom of the snake I have acquired the gentleness of the dove. I am rather sorry that I have driven away my painters and my interviewers: I have no one to inquire whom I *resemble* with my radiant countenance? I personally feel that I remind one of a powdered darkey, who is afraid to rub the powder off with his sleeve and thus reveal his black skin…ah, I still have a black skin!

Yes, I have remained *alive* but I know not yet how far I shall succeed in keeping up this state: have you any idea how hard are the transitions from a nomad to a settled life? I was a redskin, a carefree nomad, who folds up and casts off all that is human, as he would a tent. Now I am laying a granite foundation for an earthly home and I, having little faith, am cold and trembling. Will it be warm when the white snow covers my new home? What do you think, my friend, is the best heating system?

I promised Thomas Magnus that night that I would not kill myself. We sealed this agreement with a warm handshake. We did not open our veins nor seal the pact with our blood. We simply said "yes" and that was quite sufficient: as you know only human beings break agreements. Devils always keep them…. You need only recall your horny, hairy heroes and their Spartan honesty. Fortunately (let us call it 'fortunate') we had set no…date. I swear by eternal salvation, I would be a poor king and ruler if, when building a palace, I did not leave for myself a secret exit, a little door, a modest loophole through which wise kings disappear when their foolish subjects rise and break into Versailles.

I will not kill myself to-morrow. Perhaps I shall wait quite a while. I will not kill myself: of the two walls I have chosen the lower one and I am quite human now, even as you my friend. My earthly experiment is not very thrilling as yet, but who knows?—this human life may unexpectedly grow quite attractive! Has not Toppi lived to grow gray and to a peaceful end? Why should not I, traversing all the ages of man, like the seasons of the year, grow to be a gray old sage, a wise guide and teacher, the bearer of the covenant and arterio sclerosis? Ah, this ridiculous sclerosis, these ills of old age—it is only now that they begin to seem terrible to Me, but, can I not get used to them and even grow to love them? Every one says it is easy to get used to life. Well, I, too, will try to get used to it. Everything here is so well ordered that after rain comes sunshine and dries him who is wet, if he has not been in too great a hurry to die. Everything here is so well ordered that there is not a single disease for which there is no cure. This is so good! One may be ill all the time, provided there is a drug store nearby!

At any rate, I have my little door, my secret exit, my narrow, wet, dark corridor, beyond which are the stars and all the breadth of my illimitable space! My friend, I want to be frank with you: there is a certain characteristic of insubordination in me, and it is that I fear. What is a cough or a catarrh of the stomach? But it is possible that I may suddenly refuse to cough, for no reason at all, or for some trivial cause, and run off! I like you at this moment. I am quite ready to conclude a long and fast alliance with you, but *something* may suddenly gleam across your dear face which…no, it is quite impossible to do without a little secret door for him who is so capricious and insubordinate! Unfortunately, I am proud, too,—an old and well known vice of Satan! Like a fish struck in the head, I am dazed by my human existence. A fatal unconsciousness is driving me into your life, but of one thing I am quite certain: I am of the race of the *free*. I am of the tribe of the *rulers*. I come from those who transform their will into laws. Conquered kings are taken into captivity but conquered kings never become slaves. And when I shall perceive, above my head, the whip of a dirty guard and my fettered hands are helpless to avert the blow…well: shall I remain living with welts upon my back? Shall I bargain with my judges about another blow of the whip? Shall I kiss the hand of the executioner? Or shall I send to the druggist for an eye lotion?

No, let not Magnus misjudge me for a little slip in our agreement: I will live only as long as I want to live. All the blessings of the human existence, which he offered me on that night, when Satan was tempted by man, will not strike the weapon from my hand: in it alone is the assurance of my liberty! Oh, man, what are all your kingdoms and dukedoms, your knowledge and your nobility, your gold and your freedom beside this little, free movement of the finger which, in a moment carries you up to the Throne of Thrones!…

Maria!

Yes, I am afraid of her. The look in her eye is so clear and commanding, the light of her love is so mighty, enchanting and beautiful that I am all atremble and everything in me is quivering and urging me to immediate flight. With hitherto unknown happiness, with veiled promises, with singing dreams she tempts Me! Shall I cry: Away!—or shall I bend mine to her will and follow her?

Where? I do not know. Or are there other worlds beside those I know or have forgotten? Whence comes this motionless light behind my back? It is growing ever broader and brighter. Its warm touch heats my soul, so that its Polar ice crumbles and melts. But I am afraid to look back. I may see Sodom on fire and if I look I may turn into stone. Or is it a new

Sun, which I have not yet seen upon this earth that is rising behind my back, and I, like a fool, am fleeing from it and baring my back instead of my breast to it, the low, dumb neck of a frightened animal, instead of my lofty brow?

Maria! Will you give me my revolver? I paid ten dollars for it, together with the holster. To you I will not give it for a kingdom! Only do not look at Me, oh, Queen…otherwise, otherwise I will give you everything: the revolver and the holster and Satan himself!

March 26. Rome, Palazzo Orsini.
It is the fifth night that I do not sleep. When the last light is turned out in my silent palazzo, I quietly descend the stairs, quietly order a machine—somehow or other even the noise of my own steps and voice disturb me, and I go for the night into the Campagna. There, leaving the automobile on the road, I wander about until day-break or sit immovable upon some dark ruins. I cannot be seen at all and the rare passersby, perhaps some peasants from Albano, converse quite loudly and without restraint. I like to remain unseen. It reminds me of something I have forgotten.

Once, as I sat down on a stone, I disturbed a lizzard. It may have been that it lightly moved the grass beneath my feet and disappeared. Perhaps it was a snake? I do not know. But I wanted desperately to become a lizzard or a snake, concealed beneath a stone: I am troubled by my large stature, by the size of my feet and arms: They make it very difficult to become invisible. I likewise refrain from looking at my face in the mirror: it is painful to think I have a face, which all can see. Why did I fear darkness so much at the beginning? It is so easy to conceal oneself in it. Apparently all animals experience such subtle shame, fear and worriment and seek seclusion when they are changing their skin or hide.

So, I am changing my skin? Ah, it is the same, worthless prattle! The whole trouble is that I have failed to escape *Maria's* gaze and am, apparently preparing to close the last door, the door I guarded so well. But I am ashamed! I swear by eternal salvation, I feel ashamed, like a girl before the altar. I am almost blushing. Blushing Satan…no, quiet, quiet: *he* is not here! Quiet!…

Magnus told her everything. She did not reiterate that she loves Me but looked at me and said:

"Promise *me*, you will not kill yourself."

The *rest* was in her gaze. You remember how bright it is? But do not think that I hastily agreed. Like a salamander in the fire, I quickly changed colors. I shall not repeat to you all the flaming phrases I uttered: I have forgotten them. But you remember how bright and serene Maria's gaze is? I kissed her hand and said humbly:

"Madam! I do not ask you for forty days and a desert for contemplation: the desert I will find myself and a week is quite enough for me to think the matter over. But do give me a week and...please, don't look at me any more...otherwise...."

No, that wasn't what I said. I said it in other words, but it's all the same. I am now changing my skin. It hurts me. I am frightened and ashamed because any crow might see me and come to pick my flesh. What use is there in the fact that there is a revolver in my pocket? It is only when you learn to hit yourself that you can hit a crow: crows know that and consequently do not fear tragically bulging pockets.

Having become human and descended from above I have become but half a man. I entered upon this human existence as if into a strange element, but I have not lost myself in it entirely: I still cling with one hand to my Heaven and my eyes are still above the surface. But she commands me to accept man in his entirety: only he is a *man* who has said: never shall I kill myself, never shall I leave life of my own free will. And what about the whip? These cursed cuts upon my back? Pride?

Oh, Maria, Maria, how terribly you tempt Me!

I look into the past of this earth and serious myriads of tragic shadows floating slowly over climes and ages! Their hands stretch hopelessly into space, their bony ribs tear through the lean, thin skin, their eyes are filled with tears, and their sighs have dried up their throats. I see blood and madness, violence and falsehood, I hear their oaths, which they constantly betray, their prayers to God, in which, with every word of mercy and forgiveness, they curse their own earth. Wherever I look, I see the earth smoking in convulsion; no matter in which direction I strain my ear, I hear everywhere unceasing moans: or is the womb of the earth itself filled with moaning? I see a myriad cups about me, but no matter which of them my lips may touch, I find it filled with rust and vinegar: or has man no other drink? And this is *man*?

I knew *them* before. I have seen *them* before. But I looked upon them as Augustus did from his box upon the galaxy of his victims: Ave, Cæsar! These who are about to die salute you. And I looked upon them with the eyes of an eagle and my wise, belaureled head did not disdain to take notice of their groaning cries even with so much as a nod: they came and disappeared, they marched on in endless procession— and endless was the indifference of my Cæsar-like gaze. And now...is it really I who walks on so hastily, playing with the sand of the arena? And am I this dirty, emaciated, hungry slave who lifts his convict face into the air, yelling hoarsely into the indifferent eyes of Fate:

"Ave, Cæsar! Ave, Cæsar!"

I feel a sharp whip upon my back and with a cry of pain I fall to the ground. Is it some *Master* who is beating me? No, it is another *slave,* who has been ordered to whip a *slave*: very soon his knout will be in my hand and his back will be covered with blood and he will be chewing the sand, the sand which now grates between my teeth.

Oh, Maria, Maria, how terribly you tempt Me!

III

March 29 Rome.

Buy the blackest paint available, take the largest brush you can find and, with a broad line, divide my life into Yesterday and To-day. Take the staff of Moses and divide the stream of Time and dry it up clear down to its bed—then only will you sense my *To-day*.

Ave, Cæsar, moriturus te salutat!

April 2, Rome. Pallazzo Orsini.

I do not want to lie. There is not yet in me, oh man, any love for you, and if you have hastened to open your arms to me, please close them: the time has not yet come for passionate embraces. Later, at some other date, we shall embrace, but meanwhile, let us be cold and restrained, like two gentlemen in misfortune. I cannot say that my respect for you has grown to any extent, although your life and your fate have become my life and my fate: let the facts suffice that I have voluntarily placed my neck beneath the yoke and that one and the same whip are furrowing our backs.

Yes, that is quite sufficient for the present. You have observed that I no longer use a super-capital in writing the word "I"?—I have thrown it out together with the revolver. This is a sign of submission and equality. You understand? Like a king, I have taken the oath of allegiance to your constitution. But I shall not, like a king, betray this vow: I have preserved from my former life a respect for contracts. I swear I will be true to your comrades-at-hard-labor and will not make any attempt to escape alone!

For the last few nights, before I took this decision, I thought much upon *our* life. It is wretched. Don't you think so? It is difficult and humiliating to be this little thing called man, the cunning and avaricious little worm that crawls, hastily multiplies itself and lies, turning away its head from the final blow—the worm that no matter how much it lies, will perish just the same at the appointed hour. But I will be a worm. Let me, too, beget children, let the unthinking foot also crush my unthinking head at the appointed hour—I meekly accept all consequences. We are both of us humiliated, comrade, and in this alone there is some consolation: you will listen to my complaints and I—to yours. And if the matter should ultimately reach the state of litigation, why the witnesses will all be ready! That is well: When one kills in the public square there are always eyewitnesses.

I will lie, if necessary. I will not lie in that free play of lying with which even prophets lie, but in that enforced manner of lying employed by the rabbit, which compels him to hide his ears, to be gray in summer and white in winter. What can one do when behind every tree a hunter with a rifle is concealed! This lying may appear to be ignoble from one point of view and may well call forth condemnation upon us, but you and I must live, my friend. Let *bystanders* accuse us to their heart's content, but, when necessary, we will lie like wolves, too! we will spring forward, suddenly, and seize the enemy by the throat: one must live, brother, one must live, and are we to be held responsible for the fact that there is such great lure and such fine taste in blood! In reality neither you nor I are proud of our lying, of our cowardice or of our cruelty, and our bloodthirstiness is certainly not a matter of conviction.

But however hideous our life may be, it is still more miserable. Do you agree with that? I do not love you yet, oh man, but on these nights I have been more than once on the verge of tears when I thought of your suffering, of your tortured body, and of your soul, relinquished to eternal crucifixion. It is well for a wolf to be a wolf. It is well for a rabbit to be a rabbit. But you, man, contain both God and Satan—and, oh, how terrible is the imprisonment of both in that narrow and dark cell of yours! Can God be a wolf, tearing throats and drinking blood! Can Satan be a rabbit, hiding his ears behind his humped back! No, that is intolerable. I agree with you. That fills life with eternal confusion and pain and the sorrow of the soul becomes boundless.

Think of it: of three children that you beget, one becomes a murderer, the other the victim and the third, the judge and executioner. And each day the murderers are murdered and still they continue to be born; and each day the murderers kill conscience and conscience kills the murderers. And all are alive: the murderers and conscience. Oh, what a fog we live in! Give heed to all the *words* spoken by man from the day of his birth and you will think: this is God! Look at all the *deeds* of man from his very first day and you will exclaim in disgust: this is a beast! Thus does man struggle with himself for thousands of years and the sorrow of his soul is boundless and the suffering of his mind is terrible and horrible, while the *final* judge is slow about his coming…. But he will never come. I say this to you: we are forever alone with our life.

But I accept this, too. Not yet has the earth endowed me with my name and I know not who I am: Cain or Abel? But I accept the sacrifice as I do murder. I am everywhere with you and everywhere I follow you, Man. Let us weep together in the desert, knowing that no one will give heed to us…or perhaps some one will? You see: you and I are beginning to have faith in some one's Ear and soon I will begin to believe in a triangular Eye…it is really impossible that such a concert should have no hearer, that such a spectacle should be wasted on the desert air!

I think of the fact that no one has yet beaten me, and I am afraid. What will become of my soul when some one's grubby hand strikes me on the face…. What will become of me! For I know that no earthly revenge could return my face to me. And what will then become of my soul?

I swear I will become reconciled even to this. Everywhere with you and after you, man. What is my face when you struck the face of your own Christ and spat into his eyes? Everywhere with you! And if necessary, I myself will strike at Christ with the hand with which I now write: I go with you to all ends, man. They beat us and they will continue to beat us. We beat Christ and will still beat him…. Ah, bitter is our life, almost unbearable!

Only a while ago, I rejected your embraces. I said they were premature. But now I say: let us embrace more firmly, brother, let us cling closely to each other—it is so painful, so terrible to be alone in this life when all exits from it are closed. And I know not yet wherein there is more pride and liberty: in going away voluntarily, whenever one wishes, or in accepting, without resistance, the hand of the executioner? In calmly placing one's hands upon his breast, putting one foot forward and, with head proudly bent backward, to wait calmly:

"Do thy duty, executioner!"

Or:

"Soldiers, here's my breast: fire!"

There is something plastic in this pose and it pleases me. But still more am I pleased with the fact that once again my greater Ego is rising within me at the striking of this pose. Of course, the executioner will not fail to do his duty and the soldiers will not lower their rifles, but the important thing is the line, the *moment*, when before my very death itself I shall suddenly find myself immortal and broader than life itself. It is strange, but with one turn of the head, with one phrase, expressed or conceived at the proper moment, I could, so to speak, halt the function of my very spirit and the entire operation would be performed outside of me. And when death shall have finally performed its rôle of redeemer, its darkness would not eclipse the light, for the latter will have first separated itself from me and scattered into space, in order to reassemble somewhere and blaze forth again…but where?

Strange, strange…. I sought to escape from men—and found myself at that wall of Unconsciousness known only to Satan! How important, indeed, is the pose! I must make note of that. But will the pose be as convincing and will it not lose in plasticity if instead of death, the executioner and the firing squad I should be compelled to say something else… well, something like:

"Here's my face: strike!"

I do not know why I am so concerned about my face, but it does concern me greatly. I confess, man, that it worries me very much indeed. No, a mere trifle. I will simply subdue my spirit. Let them beat me! When the spirit is crushed the operation is no more painful or humiliating than it would be if I were to beat my overcoat on its hanger….

…But I have forgotten that I am not alone and being in your company have fallen into impolite meditation. For a half hour I have been silent over this sheet of paper and it seemed all the time as if I had been talking and quite excitedly! I forgot that it is not enough to think, that one must also speak! What a shame it is, man, that for the exchange of thoughts we must resort to the service of such a poor and stealthy broker as the word—he steals all that is precious and defiles the best thoughts with the chatter of the market place. In truth, this pains me much more than death or the beating.

I am terrified by the necessity of *silence* when I come upon the *extraordinary*, which is inexpressible. Like a rivulet I run and advance only as far as the ocean: in the depths of the latter is the end of my murmuring. Within me, however, motionless and omnipresent, rocking to and fro, is the ocean. It only hurls noise and surf upon the earth, but its depths are dumb and motionless and quite without any purpose are the ships sailing on its surface. How shall I describe it?

Before I resolved to enroll myself as an earthly slave I did not speak to Maria or to Magnus…. Why should I speak to Maria when her beckoning is *clear*, like her gaze? But having become a slave I went to Magnus to complain and to seek advice—apparently the human begins thus.

Magnus heard me in silence and, as it seemed to me, with some inner excitement. He works day and night, virtually knowing no rest, and the complicated business of the liquidation of my property is moving forward as rapidly in his hands as if he had been engaged in such work all his life. I like his heroic gestures and his contempt for details: when he cannot unravel a situation he hurls millions out of the window with the grace of a grandee. But he is weary and his eyes seem larger and darker on the background of his dim face. Only now have I learned from Maria that he is tortured by frequent headaches.

My complaints against life, I fear, have failed to arouse any particular sympathy on his part: No matter what the accusations I brought against man and the life he leads, Magnus would reply impatiently:

"Yes, yes, Wondergood. That is what being a man means. Your misfortune is that you discovered this rather late and are now quite unnecessarily aroused. When you shall have *experienced* at least a part of that which now terrifies you, you will speak in quite a different tone. However, I am glad that you have dropped your *indifference*: you have become, much more nervous and energetic. But whence comes this immeasurable terror in your eyes? Collect yourself, Wondergood!"

I laughed.

"Thank you. I am quite collected. Apparently it is the *slave*, in expectation of the whip, who peers at you from within my eye. Have patience, Magnus. I am not quite acclimated to the situation. Tell me, shall I or shall I not be compelled to commit…murder?"

"Quite possibly."

"And can you tell me *how* this happens?"

Both of us looked simultaneously at his white hands and Magnus replied somewhat ironically:

"No, I will not tell you that. But if you wish I will tell you something else: I will tell you what it means to accept man to the *very end*—it is this that is really worrying you, is it not?"

And with much coolness and a sort of secret impatience, as if another thought were devouring his attention, he told me briefly of a certain unwilling and terrible murderer. I do not know whether he was telling me a fact or a dark tale created for my personal benefit, but this was the story: It happened long ago. A certain Russian, a political exile, a man of wide education yet deeply religious, as often happens in Russia, escaped from *katorga*, and after long and painful wandering over the Siberian forests, he found refuge with some non-conformist sectarians. Huge, wooden, fresh huts in a thick forest, surrounded by tall fences; great bearded people, large ugly dogs—something on that order. And in his very presence, soon after his arrival, there was to be performed a monstrous crime: these insane mystics, under the influence of some wild religious fanaticism, were to sacrifice an innocent *lamb*, i.e., upon a home-made altar, to the accompaniment of hymns, they were to kill a child. Magnus did not relate all the painful details, limiting himself solely to the fact that it was a seven year old boy, in a new shirt, and that his young mother witnessed the ceremony. All the reasonable arguments, all the objections of the exile that they were about to perform a great sacrilege, that not the mercy of the Lord awaited them but the terrible tortures of hell, proved powerless to overcome the fierce and dull stubbornness of the fanatics. He fell upon his knees, begged, wept and tried to seize the knife—at that moment the victim, stripped, was already on the table while the *mother* was trying desperately to control her tears and cries—but he only succeeded in rousing the mad anger of the fanatics: they threatened to kill him, too....

Magnus looked at me and said slowly with a peculiar calm:

"And how would you have acted in that case, Mr. Wondergood?"

"Well, I would have fought until I was killed?"

"Yes! He did better. He offered his services and with his *own* hand, with appropriate song, he cut the boy's throat. You are astonished? But he said: 'Better for me to take this terrible sin and punishment upon myself than to surrender into the arms of hell these innocent fools.' Of course, such things happen only with Russians and, it seems to me, he himself was somewhat deranged. He died eventually in an insane asylum."

Following a period of silence, I asked:

"And how would you have acted, Magnus?"

And with still greater coolness, he replied:

"Really, I do not know. It would have depended on the moment. It is quite possible I would have left those beasts, but it is also possible that I too...human madness is extremely contagious, Mr. Wondergood!"

"Do you call it only madness?"

"I said: human madness. But it is you who are concerned in this, Wondergood: *how* do you like it? I am off to work. In the meantime, devote yourself to discerning the *boundary* of the human, which you are now willing to accept in its entirety, and then tell me about it. You have not changed your intention, I hope, of remaining with *us*?"

He laughed and went away, patronizingly polite. And I remained to think. And so I think: where is the boundary?

I confess that I have begun to fear Magnus somewhat...or is this fear one of the gifts of my complete human existence? But when he speaks to me in this fashion I become animated with a strange confusion, my eyes move timidly, my will is bent, as if too great and strange a load had been put upon it. Think, man: I shake his big hand with *reverence* and find *joy* in his caress! This is not true of me before, but now, in every conversation, I perceive that this man can go *further* than I in everything.

I fear I *hate* him. If I have not yet experienced love, I know not hatred either, and it will be strange indeed if I should be compelled to begin by hating the *father* of Maria!... In what a fog we do live, man! I have just merely mentioned the name of Maria, her clear gaze has only touched my soul and already my hatred of Magnus is extinguished (or did I only conjure it up?) and extinguished also is my fear of man and life (or did I merely invent it?) and great joy, great peace has descended upon me.

It is as if I were again a white schooner on the glassy ocean; as if I held all answers in my hand and were merely too lazy to open it and read therein, as if *immortality* had returned to me…ah, I can speak no more, oh, man! Let me press your hand?

April 6, 1914.

The good Toppi approves *all* my actions. He amuses me greatly, this good Toppi. As I expected, he has *completely* forgotten his true origin: he regards all my reminders of our past as jests. Sometimes he laughs but more often he frowns as if he were hurt, for he is religious and considers it an insult to be compared with a "horny" devil, even in jest: he himself is now convinced that devils have horns. His Americanism, at first pale and weak, like a pencil sketch, has now become filled with color, and I, myself, am ready to believe all the nonsense given out by Toppi as his life—it is so sincere and convincing. According to *him*, he has been in my service about fifteen years and particularly amusing it is to hear his stories of his youth.

Apparently he, too, has been touched by the charms of *Maria*: my decision to surrender all my money to her father astonished him much less than I expected. He merely chewed his cigar for a moment and asked:

"And what will he do with your money?"

"I do not know, Toppi."

He raised his brow and frowned:

"You are joking, Mr. Wondergood?"

"You see, Toppi: just now we, i.e., Magnus is occupied in converting my estate into gold and jamming it into banks, in his name, of course. You understand?"

"How can I fail to understand, Mr. Wondergood?"

"These are all preliminary, essential steps. What may happen further…I do not know yet."

"Oh, you are jesting again?"

"You must remember, old man, that I myself did not know what to do with my money. It is not money that I need but new activity. You understand? But Magnus *knows*. I do not know yet what his plans are but it is what Magnus said that is important to me: 'I will compel you to work, Wondergood!' Oh, Magnus is a great man. You will see that for yourself, Toppi!"

Toppi frowned again and replied:

"You are master of your money, Mr. Wondergood."

"Ah, you have forgotten everything, Toppi! Don't you remember about that *play*? That I wanted to play?"

"Yes, you did say something about it. But I thought you were joking."

"No, I was not joking. I was only mistaken. They do play here but this is not a theater. It is a gambling house and so I gave all my money to Magnus: let him break the bank. You understand? He is the banker, he will manage the game and I shall simply do the betting…. Quite a life, eh?"

Apparently the old fool understood nothing. He kept raising and lowering his eyebrows and again inquired:

"And how soon may we expect your betrothal to Signorina Maria?"

"I do not know yet, Toppi. But that is not the thing. I see you are dissatisfied. You do not trust Magnus?"

"Oh, Signor Magnus is a worthy man. But one thing I do fear, Mr. Wondergood, if you will permit me to be frank: he is a man who does not believe. This seems strange to me: how can the father of Signorina Maria be a non-believer? Is that not so? Permit me to ask: do you intend to give anything to his Eminence?"

"That depends now on Magnus."

"Oh! On Signor Magnus? So, so. And do you know that His Eminence has already been to see Signor Magnus? He was here a few days ago and spent several hours in this study. You were not at home at that time."

"No, I do not know. We have not spoken about that, but have no fear: we will find *something* for the cardinal. Confess, old man: you are quite enchanted with that old monkey?"

Toppi glanced at me sharply and sighed. Then he lapsed into thought…and strange as it may seem—something akin to a monkey appeared in his countenance, as in the cardinal's. Later, from somewhere deep within him, there appeared a smile. It illumined his hanging nose, rose to his eyes and blazed forth within them in two bright, little flames, not devoid of wanton malice. I looked at him in astonishment and even with joy: yes that was my old Toppi, risen from his human grave…. I am convinced that his hair again has the smell of fur instead of oil! Gently I kissed his brow—old habits cannot be rooted out—and exclaimed:

"You are enchanting, Toppi! But *what* was it that gave you such joy?"

"I waited to see whether he would show Maria to the cardinal?"

"Well?"

"He did not!"

"Well?"

But Toppi remained silent. And as it had come so did the smile disappear, slowly: at first the hanging nose grew pale and became quite in-distinct, then all at once the flames within his eyes went out—and again the old dejection, sourness and odor of church hypocrisy buried him who had been resurrected for a moment. It would have been useless to trouble the ashes with further questions.

This happened yesterday. A warm rain fell during the day but it cleared up towards evening and Magnus, weary and apparently suffering with headache, suggested that we take a ride into the Campagna. We left our chauffeur behind, a practice peculiar to all our intimate trips. His dut-ies were performed by Magnus, with extraordinary skill and daring. On this occasion, his usual daring reached the point of audacity: despite the ever-thickening twilight and the muddy road, Magnus drove the auto-mobile at such mad speed that more than once did I look up at his broad, motionless back. But that was only at first: the presence of Maria, whom I supported with my arm (I do not dare say embraced!) soon brought me to the loss of all my senses. I cannot describe it all to you—so that you would really feel it—the aromatic air of the Campagna, which caressed my face, the magnificence and charm of our arrow-like speed, my virtu-al loss of all sensation of material weight, of the complete disappearance of *body*, when I felt myself a speeding thought, a flying gaze....

But still less can I tell you of *Maria*. Her Madonna gaze whitened in the twilight, like marble; like the mysterious silence and perfect beauty of marble was her gentle, sweet and wise silence. I barely touched her slender, supple figure, but if I had been embracing within the hollow of my hand the entire firmness of earth and sky I could not have felt a more complete mastery of the *whole world*! Do you know what a line is in measurement? Not much,—is that not so? And it was only by the meas-ure of a line that Maria bent her divine form to me—no, no more than that! But what would you say, man, if the *sun*, coming down from its course just one line were to come closer to you by that distance? Would you not consider it a *miracle*?

My existence seemed unbounded, like the universe, which knows neither your time nor distance. For a moment there gleamed before me the wall of my unconsciousness, that unconquerable barrier against which the spirit of him who has donned the human form beats in vain,— and as quickly did it disappear: it was swallowed, without sound or con-flict, by the waves of my new sea. Even higher they rose, enshrouding the world. There was no longer anything to remember for me or to know: my new human soul remembered all and commanded all. I am a man!

What gave me the idea that I hate Magnus? I looked at this motion-less, erect and firm human back and thought that behind it a heart was beating. I thought of how painful and terrible it was for it to remain firm and erect and of how much pain and suffering had already fallen to the lot of this human creature, no matter how proud it might appear or dejected. And suddenly I realized to the extent of pain and tears, how much I loved Magnus, this very same Magnus! He speeds so wildly and has no fear! And the very moment I sensed this, Maria's eyes turned upon me…. Ah, they are as bright at night as they are by day! But at that moment there was a troubled look within them. They were asking: Why these tears?

What could I say in reply with the aid of weak words! I silently took Maria's hand and pressed it to my lips. And without taking her gaze off me, shining in cold, marble luster, she quietly withdrew her hand—and I became confused—and again gave it to me, taking off her glove. Will you permit me to discontinue, man? I do not know who you are, you who are reading these lines, and I rather fear you…your swift and daring imagination. Moreover, a gentleman feels ill at ease in speaking of his success with the ladies. Besides, it was time to return: on the hills the lights of Tivoli were already gleaming and Magnus reduced his speed.

We were moving quite slowly on the return trip and Magnus, grown merry, wiping his brow with his handkerchief, now and then addressed brief remarks to us. There is one thing I will not conceal: her unquestionable womanliness emphasizes the completeness of my transformation. As we walked up the broad stairs of my palazzo, amid its princely wealth and beauty, I suddenly thought:

"Why not send all this adventure to the devil? Why not simply wed and live like a prince in this palace? There will be freedom, children, laughter, just earthly happiness and love."

And again I looked at Magnus. He seemed strange to me: "I will take your money!" Then I saw the stern gaze of my Maria—and the contradiction between her love and this plan of simple, modest happiness was so great and emphatic that my thought did not even require an answer. I now recollect this thought accidentally as a curiosity of "Toppism." Let me call it "Toppism" in honor of my perfect Toppi.

The evening was charming. At Magnus' request, Maria sang. You cannot imagine the reverence with which Toppi listened to her singing! He dared not utter a word to Maria, but on leaving he shook my hand long and with particular warmth. Then, similarly, he shook the hand of Magnus. I also rose to retire.

"Do you intend to do some work yet, Magnus?"

"No. Don't you want to go to sleep, Wondergood? Come to my room. We'll chat a bit. Incidentally, there is a paper for you to sign. Do you want any wine?"

"Oh, with pleasure, Magnus. I love conversation at night."

We drank the wine. Magnus, whistling something out of tune, silently walked the carpet, while I, as usual, reclined in a chair. The Palazzo was all silence, like a sarcophagus, and this reminded me of that stirring night when Mad Mars raved behind the wall. Suddenly, Magnus exclaimed loudly, without hesitation:

"The affair is progressing splendidly."

"So?"

"In two weeks everything will be completed. Your swollen, scattered wealth, in which one can be lost as in a wood, will be transformed into a clear, concise and exact sack of gold…to be more correct—into a mountain. Do you know the exact estimate of your money, Wondergood?"

"Oh, don't, Magnus. I don't want to know it. Moreover, it's your money."

Magnus looked at me quickly and said sharply:

"No, it's yours."

I shrugged my shoulders. I did not want to argue. It was so quiet and I so enjoyed watching this strong man silently pacing to and fro. I still remembered his motionless, stern back, behind which I could clearly see his heart. He continued, after a pause:

"Do you know, Wondergood, that the Cardinal has been here?"

"The old monkey? Yes, I know. What did he want?"

"The same thing. He wanted to see you but I did not feel like taking you away from your thoughts."

"Thanks. Did you drive him out?"

Magnus replied angrily:

"I am sorry to say,—no. Don't put on airs, Wondergood: I have already told you that we must be careful of him as long as we remain here. But you are quite right. He is an old, shaven, useless, evil, gluttonous, cowardly monkey!"

"Ah, ah! Then why not show him the door?"

"Impossible."

"I believe you, Magnus. And what does this king I hear about want, he who is to visit us some of these days?"

"Ex-king. Probably the same thing. You should receive him yourself, of course."

"But only in your presence. Otherwise I refuse. You must understand, my friend, that from that memorable night on I have been merely your disciple. You find it impossible to drive out the old monkey? Very well, let him remain. You say we must receive some ex-king? Very well, receive him. But I would rather be hanged on the first lamppost than to do so without knowing your reason."

"You are jesting again, Wondergood."

"No, I am *quite* serious, Magnus. But I swear by eternal salvation that I know not what we are doing or intend to do. I am not reproaching you. I am not even questioning you: as I have already told you, I trust you and am ready to follow your directions. That you may not again reproach me with levity and impracticability, I may add a little business detail: Maria and her love are my hostages. Moreover, I do not yet know to what you intend to devote your energy, of whose boundlessness I am becoming more convinced each day; what plans and ends your experience and mind have set before you. But of one thing I have no doubt: they will be huge plans, great objects. And I, too, shall always find something to do beside you…at any rate this will be much better than my brainless old women and six secretaries. Why do you refuse to believe in my modesty, as I believe in your…genius. Imagine that I am come from some other planet, from Mars, for instance, and wish in the most serious manner possible, to pass through the experience of a *man*…. It is all very simple, Magnus!"

Magnus frowned at me for a few moments and suddenly broke into laughter:

"You certainly are a pilgrim from some other planet, Wondergood!… And what if I should devote your gold to doing evil?"

"Why? Is that so very interesting?"

"Hm!… You think *that is* not interesting?"

"Yes, and so do you. You are too big a man to do little evil, just as billions constitute too much money, while honestly as far as great evil is concerned, I know not yet what *great evil* is? Perhaps it is really *great good*? In my recent contemplations, there…came to me a strange thought: Who is of greater *use* to man—he who hates or he who loves him? You see, Magnus, how ignorant I still am of human affairs and… how ready I am for almost anything."

Without laughter and, with what seemed to me, extreme curiosity, Magnus measured me with his eyes, as if he were deciding the question: is this a fool I see before me, or the foremost sage of America? Judging by his subsequent question he was nearer the second opinion:

"So, if I have correctly understood your words, you are afraid of *nothing*, Mr. Wondergood?"

"I think *not*."

"And murder…many murders?"

"You remember the point you made in your story about the boy of the *boundary* of the human? In order that there may be no mistake, I have moved it forward several kilometers. Will that be enough?"

Something like respect arose in Magnus' eyes…the devil take him, though, he really considers me a clod! Continuing to pace the room, he looked at me curiously several times, as if he were trying to recall and verify my remark. Then, with a quick movement, he touched my shoulders:

"You have an active mind, Wondergood. It is a pity I did not come to know you before."

"Why?"

"Just so. I am interested to know how you will speak to the king: he will probably suggest something very evil to you. And great evil is great good. Is that not so?"

He again broke into laughter and shook his head in a friendly fashion.

"I don't think so. The chances are he will propose something very silly."

"Hm!... And is that not great wisdom?" He laughed again but frowned suddenly and added seriously: "Do not feel hurt, Wondergood. I liked what you said very much and it is well you do not put any questions to me at this time: I could not answer them just now. But there is something I can say even now...in general terms, of course. Are you listening?"

"I am all attention."

Magnus seated himself opposite me and, taking a sip of wine, asked with strange seriousness:

"How do you regard explosives?"

"With great respect."

"Yes? That is cold praise, but, I dare say, they don't deserve much more. Yet, there was a time when I worshiped dynamite as I do frankness...this scar on my brow is the result of my youthful enthusiasm. Since then I have made great strides in chemistry—and other things— and this has cooled my zeal. The drawback of every explosive, beginning with powder, is that the explosion is confined to a limited space and strikes only the things near at hand: it might do for war, of course, but it is quite inadequate where bigger things are concerned. Besides, being a thing of material limitations, dynamite or powder demands a constantly guiding hand: in itself, it is dumb, blind and deaf, like a mole. To be sure, in Whitehead's mine we find an attempt to create consciousness, giving the shell the power to correct, so to speak, certain mistakes and to maintain a certain aim, but that is only a pitiful parody on eyesight...."

"And you want your 'dynamite' to have consciousness, will and eyes?"

"You are right. That is what I want. And my new *dynamite* does have these attributes: will, consciousness, eyes."

"And what is your aim? But this sounds…terrible."

Magnus smiled faintly.

"Terrible? I fear your terror will turn to laughter when I give you the name of my dynamite. It is *man*. Have you never looked at man from this point of view, Wondergood?"

"I confess,—no. Does dynamite, too, belong to the domain of psychology? This is all very ridiculous."

"Chemistry, psychology!" cried Magnus, angrily: "that is all because knowledge has been subdivided into so many different subjects, just as a hand with ten fingers is now a rarity. You and your Toppi—all of us are explosive shells, some loaded and ready, others still to be loaded. And the crux of the matter lies, you understand, in how to load the shell and, what is still more important: how to explode it. You know, of course, that the method of exploding various preparations depends upon their respective compositions?"

I am not going to repeat here the lecture on explosives given me by Magnus with great zeal and enthusiasm: it was the first time I had seen him in such a state of excitement. Despite the absorbing interest of the subject, as my friends the journalists would say, I heard only half the things he was saying and concentrated most of my attention on his skull, the skull which contained such wide and dangerous knowledge. Whether it was due to the conviction carried in Magnus' words, or to pure weariness—I know not which—this round skull, blazing with the flames of his eyes, gradually assumed the character of a real, explosive shell, of a bomb, with the fuse lit for action…. I trembled when Magnus carelessly threw upon the table a heavy object resembling a cake of grayish-yellow soap, and exclaimed involuntarily:

"What's that?"

"It looks like soap or wax. But it has the force of a devil. One half of this would be enough to blow St. Peter's into bits. It is a capricious Devil. You may kick it about or chop it into pieces, you may burn it in your stove, it will remain ever silent: a dynamite shell may tear it apart yet it will not rouse its wrath. I may throw it into the street, beneath the hoofs of horses; the dogs may bite at it and children may play with it— and still it remains indifferent. But I need only apply a current of high pressure to it—and the force of the explosion will be monstrous, limitless. A strong but silly devil!"

With equal carelessness, bordering almost upon contempt, Magnus threw his devil back into the table drawer and looked at me sternly. My eyebrows twitched slightly:

"I see you know your subject to perfection, and I rather like this capricious devil of yours. But I would like to hear you discuss *man*."

Magnus laughed:

"And was it not of him I have just spoken? Is not the history of this piece of soap the history of your *man*, who can be beaten, burned, hacked to bits, hurled beneath the hoofs of horses, thrown to the dogs, torn into shreds—without rousing his consuming wrath or even his anger? But prick him with *something*—and the explosion will be terrible… as you will learn, Mr. Wondergood."

He laughed again and rubbed his white hands with pleasure: he scarcely remembered at that moment that human blood was already upon them. And is it really necessary for *man* to remember that? After a pause commensurate with the respect due to the subject, I asked:

"And do you know how to make a *man* explode?"

"Certainly."

"And would you consider it permissible to give me this information?"

"Unfortunately it is not so easy or convenient because the current of high pressure would require too much elucidation, dear Wondergood."

"Can't you put it briefly?"

"Oh, briefly. Well, it is necessary to promise man some *miracle*."

"Is that all?"

"That is all."

"Lies once more? The old monkey?"

"Yes, lies again. But not the old monkey. It is not that I have in mind. Neither crusades nor immortality in heaven. This is the period of other miracles and other wonders. He promised resurrection to the dead. I promise resurrection to the living. His followers were the dead. Mine… ours—are the living."

"But the dead *did not arise*. How about the living?"

"Who *knows*? *We must make an experiment*. I cannot yet confide in you the business end of the enterprise but I warn you: the experiment must be conducted on a very large scale. You are not afraid, Mr. Wondergood?"

I shrugged my shoulders indicating nothing definite. What could I answer? This gentleman carrying upon his shoulders a bomb instead of a head again split me into two halves, of which *man*, alas, was the lesser one. As Wondergood, I confess without shame, I felt cruel fear and even pain: just as if the monstrous explosion had already touched my bones and were now breaking them…ah, but where is my endless happiness with Maria, where the boundless peace of mind, where the devil is that white schooner? No, as Great Immortal Curiosity, as the genius of *play* and eternal movement, as the rapacious gaze of unclosing eyes I felt—I confess this, too, without shame—great joy, bordering upon ecstasy!

And with a shiver of delight I mumbled:

"What a pity I did not know that before."

"Why a pity?"

"Oh, just so. Do not forget that I am come from another planet and am only now getting acquainted with man. So what shall we do with this—planet—Magnus?"

He laughed again:

"You are a strange fellow, Wondergood! With this planet? We will give it a little holiday. But enough jesting. I do not like it!" He frowned angrily and looked at me sternly, like an old professor…the manner of this gentleman was not distinguished by flippancy. When it seemed to him that I had grown sufficiently serious he shook his head in approval and asked: "Do you know, Wondergood, that the whole of Europe is now in a very uneasy state?"

"War?"

"Possibly war. Everybody is secretly expecting it. *But* war precedes the belief in the kingdom of *miracles*. You understand: we have lived too long in simple faith in the multiplication table, *we* are tired of the multiplication table, *we* are filled with ennui and anxiety on this straight road whose mire is lost in infinity. Just now all of us are demanding some miracle and soon the day will come when we will demand the miracle immediately! It is not I alone who wants *an experiment on a large scale*—the whole world is preparing it…ah, Wondergood, in truth, life would not be worth the candle if it were not for these highly interesting moments! Highly interesting!" He greedily rubbed his hands.

"You are pleased?"

"As a chemist, I am in ecstasy. My shells are already loaded, without being themselves conscious of the fact, but they will know it well enough when I apply the torch. Can you imagine the sight when *my* dynamite will begin to explode, its consciousness, its will, its eyes directed straight upon its goal?"

"And blood? Perhaps my reminder is out of place but I remember an occasion when you spoke of *blood* with much excitement."

Magnus fixed his long gaze upon me: something akin to suffering appeared in his eyes: But this was not the prick of conscience or pity—it was the emotion of a mature and wise man whose thoughts had been interrupted by the foolish question of a child: "Blood," he said, "what blood?"

I recalled to him his words on that occasion and told him of my strange and extremely unpleasant dream about the bottles, filled with blood instead of wine, and so easily broken. Weary, with his eyes closed, he listened to my tale and sighed heavily.

"Blood!"—he murmured: "blood! that's nonsense. I told you many trite things on that occasion, Wondergood, and it is not worth while to recall them. However, if *this* gives you fear, it is not too late."

I replied resolutely:

"I fear *nothing*. As I have already said, I shall follow you everywhere. It is *my* blood that is protesting—you understand?—not my consciousness or will. Apparently I shall be the first to be fooled by you: I, too, seek a miracle. Is not your *Maria* a miracle? I have been repeating the multiplication table night and day and I have grown to hate it like the bars of a prison. From the point of view of your chemistry, I am quite loaded and I ask but one thing: blow me up as quickly as possible!"

Magnus agreed sternly:

"Very well. In about two weeks. Are you satisfied?"

"Thank you. I hope that Signorina Maria will then become my wife?"

Magnus laughed.

"Madonna?"

"Oh, I don't understand your smile…and, I must say, my hope is altogether in conformity with the regard I bear for your daughter, Signor Magnus."

"Don't excite yourself, Wondergood. My smile was not about Maria but about your faith in miracles. You are a splendid fellow, Wondergood. I am beginning to love you like a son. In two weeks you will receive everything and then we shall conclude a new and strong pact. Your hand, comrade!"

For the first time he shook my hand in a strong, comradely fashion. I would have kissed him if there had been a simple human head instead of a bomb upon his shoulders. But to touch a bomb! Not even in the face of my utmost respect for him!

That was the first night that I slept like one slain and the stone walls of the palace did not press upon me. The walls were brushed by the explosive power of Magnus' speech, while the roof melted away beneath the starry coverlet of Maria: my soul departed into the realms of her calm love and refuge. The mountain Tivoli and its fires—that was what I saw as I fell into slumber.

April 8, Rome.

Before knocking at my door, His Majesty, the ex-King E. had knocked at no small number of entrances in Europe. True to the example of his apostolic ancestors, who believed in the gold of Israel, he particularly liked to approach Jewish bankers; I believe that the honor done me by his visit was based upon his firm conviction that I was a Jew. Although His Majesty was visiting Rome incognito, I, warned of his visit, met him at the foot of the stairs and bowed low to him—I think that is the requirement of etiquette. Then, also in accordance with etiquette, we introduced ourselves, he—his adjutant, I—Thomas Magnus.

I confess I had not a very flattering opinion of the former king and that is why he astonished me all the more with his high opinion of himself. He gave me his hand politely but with such haughty indifference, he looked at me with such complete self-confidence, as if he were gazing at a being of a lower order, he walked ahead of me so naturally, sat down without invitation, gazed upon the walls and furniture in such frankly royal manner, that my entire uneasiness due to my unfamiliarity with etiquette disappeared immediately. It was only necessary to follow this fellow, who appeared to know everything so well. In appearance he was quite a young man, with fresh complexion and magnificent coiffure, somewhat worn out but sufficiently well-preserved, with colorless eyes and a calm, brazenly protruding lower lip. His hands were beautiful. He did not try to conceal that he was bored by my American face, which appeared Jewish to him, and by the necessity of asking me for money: he yawned slightly after seating himself and said:

"Sit down, gentlemen."

And with a slight command of the hand he ordered the adjutant to state the nature of his proposal. He paid no attention to Magnus at all, and while the fat, red and obliging adjutant was stealthily narrating the story of the "misunderstanding" which caused the departure of His Majesty from his country—His Majesty was nonchalantly examining his feet. Finally, he interrupted his representative's speech with the impatient remark:

"Briefer, Marquis. Mr…. Wondergood is as well familiar with this history as we are. In a word, these fools kicked me out. How do you regard it, dear Wondergood?"

"How do I regard it?" I bowed low:

"I am glad to be of service to Your Majesty."

"Well, yes, that's what they all say. But will you give me any money? Continue, Marquis."

The Marquis, smiling gently at me and Magnus (despite his obesity he looked quite hungry) continued to weave his thin flimsy web about the misunderstanding, until the bored king again interrupted him:

"You understand: these fools thought that I was responsible for all their misfortunes. Wasn't that silly, Mr. Wondergood? And now they are worse off than ever and they write: 'Come back, for God's sake. We are perishing!' Read the letters, Marquis."

At first the king spoke with a trace of excitement but apparently any effort soon wearied him. The Marquis obediently took a packet of papers from the portfolio and tortured us with the complaints of the orphaned subjects, begging their lord to return. I looked at the king: he was no less bored than we were. It was so clear to him that the people could not exist without him that all confirmations of this seemed superfluous.... And I felt so strange: whence does this miserable man get so much happy confidence? There was no doubt that this bird, unable to find a crumb for himself, sincerely believed in the peculiar qualities of his personage, capable of bestowing upon a whole people marvelous benefactions. Stupidity? Training? Habit? At that moment the marquis was reading the plea of some correspondent, in which, through the web of official mediocrity and the lies of swollen phrases, gleamed the very same confidence and sincere call. Was that, too, stupidity and habit?

"And so forth, and so forth," interrupted the king listlessly: "that will do, Marquis, you may close your portfolio. Well, what you think of it, dear Mr. Wondergood?"

"I will be bold enough to say to Your Majesty that I am a representative of an old, democratic republic and...."

"Stop, Wondergood! Republic, democracy! That's nonsense. You know well enough yourself that a king is a necessity. You, in America, will have a king, too, some day. How can you get along without a king: who will be responsible for them before God? No, that's foolish."

This creature was actually getting ready to answer for the people before God! And he continued with the same calm audacity:

"The king can do everything. And what can a president do? Nothing. Do you understand, Wondergood—*Nothing*! Why, then, do you want a president who can do nothing?"—he deigned to twist his lower lip into a sarcastic smile.—"It is all nonsense, invented by the newspapers. Would you, for example, take your president seriously, Mr. Wondergood?"

"But representative government...."

"Fi! Excuse me, Mr. Wondergood (he recalled my name with great difficulty) but what fool will pay any attention to the representatives of the people? Citizen A will pay heed to Citizen B and Citizen B will pay heed to Citizen A—is that not so? But who will compel their obedience if both of them are wise? No, I, too, have studied logic, Mr. Wondergood and you will permit me to indulge in a laugh!"

He laughed slightly and said with his usual gesture:

"Continue, Marquis.... No, let me do it. The King can do *everything*, Wondergood, you understand?"

"But the law...."

"Ah, this fellow, too, speaks of law. Do you hear, Marquis? No, I really can't understand what you want this law for! That all may suffer equitably! However, if you are so keen on having law, law you shall have. But who will give it to you, if not I?"

"But the representatives of the people...."

The king directed his colorless eyes upon me, almost in despair:

"Ah, again citizen A and B! But can't you understand, dear Wondergood? What kind of a law is it if they themselves make it? What wise man will agree to obey it? No, that's nonsense. Is it possible that you yourself obey this law, Wondergood?"

"Not only I, Your Majesty, but the whole of America...."

His eyes measured me with sympathy.

"Pardon me, but I don't believe it. The whole of America! Well, in that case they simply don't understand what law is—do you hear, Marquis, the whole of America! But that's not the thing. I must return, Wondergood. You've heard what the poor devils write?"

"I am happy to see that the road is open for you, my lord."

"Open? You think so? Hm! No, I need money. Some write and others don't, you understand?"

"Perhaps they don't know how to write, my lord?"

"They? Oh! You should have seen what they wrote against me. I was quite flustered. What they need is the firing squad."

"All of them?"

"Why all of them? Some of them will be enough. The rest of them will simply be scared to death. You understand, Wondergood, they have simply stolen my power from me and now, of course, will simply refuse to return it. You can't expect me to see to it that no one robs me. And these gentlemen,"—he indicated the blushing Marquis—"to my sorrow did not manage to guard my interests."

The Marquis mumbled confusedly:

"Sire!"

"Now, now, I know your devotion, but you were asleep at the switch just the same? And now there is so much trouble, so much trouble!"—he sighed lightly. "Did not Cardinal X. tell you I needed money, Mr. Wondergood? He promised to. Of course I will return it all and...however, you should take this matter up with the Marquis. I have heard that you love people very much, Mr. Wondergood?"

A faint smile flitted over the dim face of Magnus. I bowed slightly.

"The Cardinal told me so. That is very praiseworthy, Mr. Wondergood. But if you do love people you will certainly give me money. I don't doubt that in the least. They must have a king. The newspapers are merely prattling nonsense. Why do they have a king in Germany, a king in England, a king in Italy, and a hundred other kings? And don't we need a king too?"

The adjutant mumbled:

“A misunderstanding....”

“Of course a misunderstanding. The Marquis is quite right. The newspapers call it a revolution, but believe me, I know my people; it is simply a misunderstanding. They are now weeping themselves. How can they get along without a king? There would be no kings at all then. You understand? What nonsense! They now talk of no God, too. No, we must do a little shooting, a little shooting!”

He rose quickly and this time shook my hand with a patronizing smile and bowed to Magnus.

“Good-by, good-by, my dear Wondergood. You have a magnificent figure.... Oh, what a splendid fellow! The Marquis will drop in to see you one of these days. There was something more I wanted to say. Oh, yes: I hope that you in America will have a king, too, in the near future... that is very essential, my friend. Moreover, that’s bound to be the end! Au revoir!”

We escorted His Majesty with the same ceremony. The Marquis followed and his bowed head, divided into two halves by the part in his reddish hair, and his red face bore the expression of hunger and constant failure.... Ah, he has so frequently and so fruitlessly orated about that ‘misunderstanding’! The King, apparently, also recalled at that moment his vain knocking about at other thresholds: his bloodless face again filled with grayish ennui and in reply to my parting bow, he opened wide his eyes, as if in astonishment, with the expression: what more does this fool want? Ah, yes, he has money. And lazily he asked:

“And so, you’ll not forget, Mr....friend!” And his automobile was magnificent and just as magnificent was the huge chauffeur, resembling a gendarme, attired for the new rôle. When we had reascended the stairs (our respectful lackeys meanwhile gazing upon me as on a royal personage) and entered our apartments, Magnus fell into a long, ironic silence. I asked:

“How old is this creature?”

“Didn’t you know, Wondergood? That’s bad. He is 32 years old. Perhaps less.”

“Did the Cardinal really speak of him and ask you to give him money?”

“Yes,—from what you may have left after the Cardinal’s wants are attended to.”

“That is probably due to the fact that the monarchist form of government is also in vogue in heaven. Can you conceive of a republic of saints and the administration of the world on the basis of popular representation? Think of it: even devils will then receive the vote. A King is most necessary, Wondergood. Believe me.”

"Nonsense! This is not worthy even of a jest."

"I am not jesting. You are mistaken. And pardon me for being so direct, my friend: in his discussion about kings *he* was above you, this time. You saw only a creature, a countenance of purely material limitations and ridiculous. *He* conceived himself to be a symbol. That is why he is so calm and there is no doubt that he will return to his beloved people."

"And will do a little shooting."

"And will do a little shooting. And will throw a little scare into them. Ah, Wondergood, how stubborn you are in your refusal to part with the multiplication table! Your republic is a simple table, while a king— do you realize it?—is a *miracle*! What can there be simpler, sillier and more hopeless than a million bearded men, governing themselves,—and how wonderful, how miraculous when this million of bearded fellows are governed by a creature! That is a miracle! And what possibilities it gives rise to! It seemed very funny to me when you spoke with so much warmth about the law, this dream of the devil. A king is necessary for the precise purpose of *breaking* the law, in order that the *will* may be *above* the law!"

"But laws change, Magnus."

"To change is only to submit to necessity and to new law, which was unknown to you before. Only by breaking the law do you elevate the *will*. Prove to me that God himself is subject to his own laws, i.e., to put it simply, that he cannot perform miracles, and to-morrow your shaven monkey will share the fate of loneliness and all the churches will be turned into horse stables. The miracle, Wondergood, the miracle—that is what holds human beings on this cursed earth!"

Magnus emphasized these words by banging the table with his fist. His face was gloomy. In his dark eyes there flickered unusual excitement. Speaking as if he were threatening some one, he continued:

"*He* believes in miracles and I envy him. He is insignificant, he is really what you might call a creature, but he believes in miracles. And he has already been a king and will be a king again! And we!..."

He waved his hand contemptuously and began to pace the carpet like an angry captain on the deck of *his* vessel. With much respect I gazed upon his heavy, explosive head and blazing eyes: for the first time I realized what *Satanic* ambitions there were concealed in this strange gentlemen. "And we!" Magnus noticed my gaze and shouted angrily:

"Why do you look at me like that, Wondergood? It's silly! You are thinking of my ambition? That's foolish, Wondergood! Would not *you*, a gentleman of Illinois, also like to be...well, at least, Emperor of *Russia*, where the *will* is still above the law?"

"And on what particular throne have you your eye, Magnus?" I replied, no longer concealing my irony.

"If you are pleased to think of me so flatteringly, Wondergood, I will tell you that I *aim* much higher. Nonsense, my friend! Only bloodless moralists have never dreamt of a crown, just as only eunuchs have never tempted themselves with the thought of woman. Nonsense! But I do not seek a throne—not even the Russian throne: it is too cramping."

"But there is another throne, Signor Magnus: the throne of God."

"But why only the throne of God? And have you forgotten Satan's, Mr. Wondergood?"

And this he said to Me…or did the whole street know that my throne was vacant? I bowed my head respectfully and said:

"Permit me to be the first to greet you…Your Majesty."

Magnus turned on me in wild wrath, gnashing his teeth, like a dog over a contested bone. And this angry atom wants to be Satan! This handful of earth, hardly enough for one whiff for the Devil, is dreaming to be crowned with my crown! I bowed my head still lower and dropped my eyes: I felt the gleaming flame of contempt and divine laughter blazing forth within them. I realized that it must not be given to my honored ward to know this *laughter*. I do not know how long we remained silent, but when our eyes met again they were clear, pure and innocent, like two bright rays in the shade. Magnus was the first to speak:

"And so?" he said.

"And so?" I replied.

"Will you order money for the king?"

"The money is at your disposal, my dear friend."

Magnus looked at me thoughtfully.

"It's not worth while," he decided. "This miracle is old stuff. It requires too many police to compel belief. We shall perform a better miracle."

"Oh, undoubtedly. We shall contrive a better device. In two weeks?"

"Yes, about that!" replied Magnus cordially.

We shook hands warmly in parting and in about two hours the gracious king sent each of us a decoration: some sort of a star for me and something else for Magnus. I rather pitied the poor idiot who continued to play his lone hand.

April 16, Rome.

Maria is somewhat indisposed and I hardly see her. Magnus informed me of her illness—and lied about it: for some reason he does not want me to see her. Does he fear anything?

Again Cardinal X. called on him in my absence. Nothing is being said to me about the "miracle."

But I am patient,—and I wait. At first this was rather boresome but recently I have found a new pastime and now I am quite content. It is the Roman museums, where I spend my mornings, like a conscientious American who has just learned to distinguish between a painting and a piece of sculpture. But I have no Baedecker with me and I am strangely happy that I don't understand a thing about it all: marble and painting. I merely like it.

I like the odor of the sea in the museums. Why the sea?—I do not know: the sea is far away and I rather expected the odor of decay. And it is so spacious here—much more spacious than the Campagna. In the Campagna I see only space, over which run trains and automobiles. Here I swim in time. There is so much time here! Then, too, I rather like the fact that here they preserve with great care a chip of a marble foot or a stony sole with a bit of the heel. Like an ass from Illinois, I simply cannot understand what value there is in this, but I already believe that it is valuable and I am touched by your careful thrift, little man! Preserve it! Go on breaking the feet of live men. That is nothing. But these you must preserve. It is good, indeed, when living, dying, ever changing men, for the space of 2000 years, take such good care of a chip of marble foot.

When I enter the narrow museum from the Roman street, where every stone is drowned in the light of the April sun, its transparent and even shadow seems to me a peculiar light, more durable than the expensive rays of the sun. As far as I *recollect* it is thus that eternity doth shine. And these marbles! They have swallowed as much sunlight as an Englishman whiskey before they were driven into this place that they do not fear night at all…. And I, too, do not fear the night when I am near them. Take care of them, man!

If *this* is what you call art, what an ass you are, Wondergood. Of course, you are cultured, you look upon art with reverence as upon religion and you have understood as much of it as that ass did on which the Messiah entered Jerusalem. And what if there should be a fire? Yesterday this thought troubled me all day and I went with it to Magnus. But he seems extremely occupied with something and could not, at first, understand what I was driving at.

"What's the trouble, Wondergood? You want to insure the Vatican—or something else? Make it clearer?"

"Oh! to insure!" I exclaimed in anger: "you are a barbarian, Thomas Magnus!"

At last he understood. Smiling cordially, he stretched, yawned and laid some paper before me.

"You really are a gentleman from Mars, dear Wondergood. Don't contradict, and sign this paper. It is the last one."

"I will sign, but under one condition. Your explosion must not touch the Vatican."

He laughed again:

"Would you be sorry? Then you had better not sign. In general, if you are sorry about anything—about anything at all—it would be better for us to part before it is too late. There is no room for pity in my game and my play is not for sentimental American girls."

"If you please...." I signed the paper and threw it aside. "But it seems as if you have earnestly entered upon the duties of Satan, dear Magnus!"

"And does Satan have duties? Poor Satan! Then I don't want to be Satan!"

"Neither duties nor obligations?"

"Neither duties nor obligations."

"And what then?"

He glanced at me quickly with his gleaming eyes and replied with one short word, which cut the air before my face:

"*Will.*"

"And...the current of high pressure?"

Magnus smiled patronizingly:

"I am very glad that you remember my words so well, Wondergood. They may be of use to you some day."

Cursed dog. I felt so much like striking him that I—bowed particularly low and politely. But he restrained me with a gracious gesture, pointing to a chair:

"Where are you going, Wondergood? Sit down. We have seen so little of each other of late. How is your health?"

"Fine, thank you. And how is the health of Signorina Maria?"

"Not particularly good. But it's a trifle. A few more days of waiting and you.... So you like the museums, Wondergood? There was a time when I, too, gave them much time and feeling. Yes, I remember, I remember.... Don't you find, Wondergood, that man, in mass, is a repulsive being?"

I raised my eyes in astonishment:

"I do not quite understand this change of subject, Magnus. On the contrary, the museums have revealed to me a new and more attractive side of man...."

He laughed.

"Love for mankind?... Well, well, do not take offense at the jest, Wondergood. You see: everything that man does in crayon is wonderful—but repulsive in painting. Take the sketch of Christianity, with its sermon on the Mount, its lilies and its ears of corn, how marvelous it is! And how ugly is its picture with its sextons, its funeral pyres and its Cardinal X.! A genius begins the work and an idiot, an animal, completes it. The pure and fresh wave of the ocean tide strikes the dirty shore—and returns dirty, bearing back with it corks and shells. The beginning of love, the beginning of the Roman Empire and the great revolution—how good are all beginnings! And their end? And even if a man here and there has managed to die as beautifully as he was born, the masses, the masses, Wondergood, invariably end the liturgy in shamelessness!"

"Oh, but what about the causes, Magnus?"

"The causes? Apparently we find concealed here the very *substance* of man, of animal, evil and limited in the mass, inclined to madness, easily inoculated with all sorts of disease and crowning the widest possible road with a standstill. And that is why Art is so much above Man!"

"I do not understand."

"*What* is there incomprehensible about it? In art it is the genius who begins and the genius completes. You understand: the genius! the fool, the imitator or the critic is quite powerless to change or mar the paintings of Velasquez, the sculpture of Angelo or the verse of Homer. He can destroy, smash, break, burn or deface, but he is quite powerless to bring them down to his own level—and that is why he so detests real art. You understand, Wondergood? His paw is helpless!"

Magnus waved his white hand and laughed.

"But why does he guard and protect it so assiduously?"

"It is not *he* who guards and protects. This is done by a special species of *faithful watchmen*"—Magnus laughed again: "and did you observe how uncomfortable they feel in the museum?"

"Who—they?"

"Well, those who came to view the things! But the most ridiculous phase of the whole business is not that the fool is a fool but that the genius unswervedly worships the fool as a neighbor and fellow being and anxiously seeks his devastating love. As if he were a savage himself, the genius does not understand that *his* true neighbor is a genius similar to himself and he is eternally opening his embraces to the near—human…who eagerly crawls into them in order to abstract the watch from his vest pocket! Yes, my dear Wondergood, it is a most laughable point and I fear…."

He lapsed into thought, fixing his eyes upon the floor: thus apparently do human beings gaze into the depths of their own graves. And I understood just what this genius feared, and once again I bowed before the Satanic mind which in all the world recognized only itself and its own will. Here was a god who would not share his power with Olympus! And what a contempt for mankind! And what open contempt for me! Here was a grain of earth that could make the devil himself sneeze!

And do you know how I concluded that evening? I took my pious Toppi by the neck and threatened to shoot him if he did not get drunk with me. And drunk we did get! We began in some dirty little café and continued in some night taverns where I generously filled some black-eyed bandits with liquor, mandolin players and singers, who sang to me of Maria: I drank like a farm hand who had just arrived in the city after a year of sober labor. Away with the museums! I remember that I shouted much and waved my hands—but never did I love my *Maria* so tenderly, so sweetly and so painfully as in that smoke of drink, permeated with the odor of wine, oranges and some burning fat, in this wide circle of black bearded stealthy faces and rapaciously gleaming eyes, amid the melodious strains of mandolins which opened for me the very vestibules of heaven and hell!

I vaguely remember some very accommodating but pompous murderers, whom I kissed and forgave in the name of Maria. I remember that I proposed that all of us go to drink in the Coliseum, in the very place where martyrs used to die but I do not know why we did not do it—I believe there were technical difficulties. And how splendid Toppi was! At first he drank long and silently, like an archbishop. Then he suddenly began to perform interesting feats. He put a bottle of Chianti on his nose, the wine running all over him. He tried to perform some tricks with cards but was immediately caught by the affable bandits who brilliantly repeated the same trick. He walked on all fours and sang some religious verses through his nose. He cried and suddenly announced frankly that he was a devil.

We walked home staggering along the street, bumping into walls and lampposts and hilariously enjoying ourselves like two students. Toppi tried to pick a quarrel with some policemen, but, touched by their politeness, he ended by conferring his stern blessing upon them, saying gloomily:

"Go and sin no more."

Then he confessed with tears that he was in love with a certain signorina, that his love was requited and that he must therefore resign his spiritual calling. Saying this, he lay down upon a stony threshold and fell into a stubborn sleep. And thus I left him.

Maria, Maria, how you tempt me! Not once have I touched your lips. Yesterday I kissed only red wine…but whence come these burning traces on my lips? But yesterday I stood upon my knees, Madonna, and covered you with flowers: but yesterday I timidly laid hands upon the hem of your garment, and to-day you are only a woman and I want you. My hands are trembling. The obstacles, the halls, the paces and the thresholds separating us drive me mad. I want you! I did not recognize my own eyes in the mirror: there is a thick shadow upon them. I breathe heavily and irregularly, and all day long my thoughts are wandering lustfully about your naked breast. I have forgotten everything.

In whose power am I? It bends me like soft, heated iron. I am deafened, I am blinded by my own heat and sparks. What do you do, man, when *that* happens to you? Do you simply go and take the woman? Do you violate her? Think: it is night now and Maria is so close by. I can approach her room without a sound…and I want to hear her cries! But suppose Magnus bars the road for me? I will kill Magnus.

Nonsense.

No, tell me, in whose power am I? You ought to know that man? To-day, just before evening, as I was seeking to escape from myself and Maria, I wandered about the streets, but it was worse there: everywhere I saw men and women, men and women. As if I had never seen them before! They all appeared naked to me. I stood long at Monte-Picio and tried to grasp what a sunset was but could not: before me there passed by in endless procession those men and women, gazing into each other's eyes. Tell me—what is Woman? I saw one—very beautiful—in an automobile. The sunset threw a rosy glow upon her pale face and in her ears there glistened two diamond sparks. She gazed upon the sunset and the sunset gazed on her, but I could not endure it: sorrow and love gripped my heart, as if I were dying. There behind her were trees, green, almost black.

Maria! Maria!

April 19, Isle of Capri.
Perfect calm reigned upon the sea. From a high precipice I gazed long upon a little schooner, motionless in the blue expanse. Its white sails were rigidly still and it seemed as happy as on that memorable day. And, again, great calm descended upon me, while the holy name of *Maria* resounded purely and peacefully, like the Sabbath bells on the distant shore.

There I lay upon the grass, my face toward the sky. The good earth warmed my back, while my eyes were pierced with warm light, as if I had thrust my face into the sun. Not more than three paces away there lay an abyss, a steep precipice, a dizzying wall, and it was delightful to imbibe the odor of grass and the Spring flowers of Capri. There was also the odor of Toppi, who was lying beside me: when he is heated by the sun he emits the smell of fur. He was all sunburned, just as if he had been smeared with coal. In general, he is a very amiable old Devil.

The place where we lay is called Anacapri and constitutes the elevated part of the island. The sun had already set when we began our trip downward and a half moon had risen in the sky. But there was the same quiet and warmth and from somewhere came the strains of mandolins in love, calling to Maria. Maria everywhere! But my love breathed with great calm, bathed in the pure moonlight rays, like the little white houses below. In such a house, at one time, did Maria live, and into just such a house I will take her in about four days.

A high wall along which the road ran, concealed the moon from us and here we beheld the statue of an old Madonna, standing in a niche, high above the road and the surrounding bushes. Before her burned with a weak flame the light of an image-lamp, and she seemed so alive in her watchful silence that my heart grew cold with sweet terror. Toppi bowed his head and mumbled a prayer, while I removed my hat and thought:

How high above this earthly vessel, filled with moonlit twilight and mysterious charms, you stand. Thus does *Maria* stand above my soul....

Enough! Here again the extraordinary begins and I must pause. We shall soon drink some champagne and then we shall go to the café. I understand they expect some mandolin players from Naples there to-day. Toppi would rather be shot than follow me: his conscience troubles him to this day. But it is good that I will be alone.

April 23—Rome, Palazzo Orsini.

...Night. My palace is dead and silent, as if it were one of the ruins of ancient Rome. Beyond the large window lies the garden: it is transparent and white with the rays of the moon and the vaporous pole of the fountain resembles a headless vision in a silver veil. Its splash is scarcely heard through the thick window-pane—as if it were the sleepy mumbling of the night guard.

Yes, this is all beautiful and...how do you put it?—it breathes with love. Of course, it would be good to walk beside Maria over the blue sand of the garden path and to trample upon her shadow. But I am disturbed and my disquiet is wider than love. In my attempts to walk lightly I wander about the room, lean against the wall, recline in silence in the corners, and all the time I seem to hear something. Something far away, a thousand kilometers from here. Or is this all lodged in my memory— that which I strain my ear to catch? And the thousand kilometers—are they the thousand years of my life?

You would be astonished if you saw how I was dressed. My fine American costume had suddenly become unbearably heavy, so I put on my bathing suit. This made me appear thin, tall and wiry. I tried to test my nimbleness by crawling about the floor, suddenly changing the direction, like a noiseless bat. But it is not I who am restless. It is my muscles that are filled with this unrest, and I know not what they want. Then I began to feel cold. I dressed and sat down to write. I drank some wine and drew down the curtains to shut the white garden from my eyes. Then

I examined and fixed my Browning. I intend to take it with me to-morrow for a friendly chat with Magnus.

You see, Thomas Magnus has some *collaborators*. That is what he calls those gentlemen unknown to me who respectfully get out of my way when we meet, but never greet me, as if we were meeting in the street and not in my house. There were two of them when I went to Capri. Now they are six, according to what Toppi tells me, and they live here. Toppi does not like them. Neither do I. They seem to have no *faces*. I could not see them. I happened to think of that just now when I tried to recall them.

"These are my assistants," Magnus told me to-day without trying in the least to conceal his ridicule.

"Well, I must say, Magnus, they have had bad training. They never greet me when we meet."

"On the contrary, dear Wondergood! They are very well-mannered. They simply cannot bring themselves to greet you without a proper introduction. They are…extremely correct people. However, you will learn all to-morrow. Don't frown. Be patient, Wondergood! Just one more night!"

"How is Signorina Maria's health?"

"*To-morrow* she will be well." He placed his hand upon my shoulder and brought his dark, evil, brazen eyes closer to my face: "The passion of love, eh?"

I shook off his hand and shouted:

"Signor Magnus! I…."

"You?"—he frowned at me and calmly turned his back upon me: "Till to-morrow, Mr. Wondergood!"

That is why I loaded my revolver. In the evening I was handed a letter from Magnus: he begged my pardon, said his conduct was due to unusual excitement and he sincerely sought my friendship and confidence. He also agreed that his *collaborators* are really ill-mannered folk. I gazed long upon these hasty illegible lines and felt like taking with me, not my revolver, but a cannon.

One more night, but how long it is!

There is danger facing me.

I feel it and my muscles *know* it, too. Do you think that I am merely afraid? I swear by eternal salvation—no! I know not where my fear has disappeared, but only a short while ago I was afraid of everything: of darkness, death and the most inconsequential pain. And now I fear nothing. I only feel strange…is that how you put it: strange?

Here I am on your earth, man, and I am thinking of another person who is dangerous to me and I myself am—man. And there is the moon and the fountain. And there is Maria, whom I love. And here is a glass and wine. And this is—my and your life. Or did I simply imagine that I was Satan once? I see *it* is all an invention, the fountain and Maria and my very thoughts on the man—Magnus, but the *real* my mind can neither unravel nor understand. I assiduously examine my memory and it is silent, like a closed book, and I have no power to open this enchanted volume, concealing the whole past of my being. Straining my eyesight, I gaze into the bright and distant depth from which I came upon this pasteboard earth—but I see nothing in the painful ebb and flow of the boundless fog. There, behind the fog, is my country, but it seems—it seems I have quite forgotten the road.

I have again returned to Wondergood's bad habit of getting drunk alone and I am slightly drunk now. No matter. It is the last time. I have just seen something after which I wish to see nothing else. I felt like taking a look at the white garden and to imagine how it would feel to walk beside Maria over the path of blue sand. I turned off the light in the room and opened wide the draperies. And the white garden arose before me, like a dream, and—think of it!—over the path of blue sand there walked a man and a woman—and the woman was Maria! They walked quietly, trampling upon their own shadows, and the man embraced her. The little counting machine in my breast beat madly, fell to the floor and broke, when, finally, I recognized the man—it was Magnus, only Magnus, dear Magnus, the father. May he be cursed with his fatherly embraces!

Ah, how my love for *Maria* surged up again within me! I fell on my knees before the window and stretched out my hands to her…. To be sure, I had already seen something of that kind in the theater, but it's all the same to me: I stretched out my hands—was I not alone and drunk! Why should I not do what I want to do? Madonna! Then I suddenly drew down the curtain!

Quietly, like a web, like a handful of moonlight, I will take this vision and weave it into night dreams. Quietly!… Quietly!…

IV

May 25, 1914.—Italy.

Had I at my disposal, not the pitiful word but a strong orchestra, I would compel all the brass trumpets to roar. I would raise their blazing mouths to the sky and would compel them to rave incessantly in a blazen, screeching voice which would make one's hair stand on end and scatter the clouds in terror. I do not want the lying violins. Hateful to me is the gentle murmur of false strings beneath the fingers of liars and scoundrels. Breath! Breath! My gullet is like a brass horn. My breath—a hurricane, driving forward into every narrow cleft. And all of me rings, kicks and grates like a heap of iron in the face of the wind. Oh, it is not always the mighty, wrathful roar of brass trumpets. Frequently, very frequently it is the pitiful wail of burned, rusty iron, crawling along lonely, like the winter, the whistle of bent twigs, which drives thought cold and fills the heart with the rust of gloom and homelessness. Everything that fire can touch has burned up within me. Was it I who wanted to play? Was it I who yearned for the game? Then—look upon this monstrous ruin of the theater wrecked by the flames: all the actors, too, have lost their lives therein.. ah, all the actors, too, have perished, and brazen Truth peers now through the beggarly holes of its empty windows.

By my throne,—what was that love I prattled of when I donned this human form? To whom was it that I opened my embraces? Was it you… comrade? By my throne!—if I was Love but *for a single moment*, henceforth I am Hate and *eternally* thus I remain.

Let us halt at this point to-day, dear comrade. It has been quite some time since I moved my pen upon this paper and I must now grow accustomed anew to your dull and shallow face, smeared o'er with the red of your cheeks. I seem to have forgotten how to speak the language of respectable people who have just received a trouncing. Get thee hence, my friend. To-day I am a brass trumpet. Tickle not my throat, little worm. Leave me.

May 26, Italy.

It was a month ago that Thomas Magnus *blew* me up. Yes, it is true. He really blew me up and it was a month ago, in the holy City of Rome, in the Palazzo Orsini, when I still belonged to the billionaire Henry Wondergood—do you remember that genial American, with his cigar and patent gold teeth? Alas! He is no longer with us. He died suddenly and you will do well if you order a requiem mass for him: his Illinois soul is in need of your prayers.

Let us return, however, to his last hours. I shall try to be exact in My recollections and give you not only the emotions but also the words of that evening—it was evening, when the moon was shining brightly. Perhaps I shall not give you quite the words spoken but, at any rate, they will be the words I heard and stored away in my memory…. If you were ever whipped, worthy comrade, then you know how difficult it was for you to count all the blows of the whip. A change of gravity! You understand? Oh, you understand everything. And so let us receive the last breath of Henry Wondergood, blown up by the culprit Thomas Magnus and buried by…*Maria.*

I remember: I awoke on the morning after that *stormy* evening, calm and even gay. Apparently it was the effect of the sun, shining into that same, broad window through which, at night, there streamed that unwelcome and too highly significant moonlight. You understand: now the moon and now the sun? Oh, you understand everything. It is probably for the very same reason I acquired my touching faith in the integrity of Magnus and awaited toward evening that cloudless bliss. This expectation was all the greater because his collaborators…you remember his collaborators?—had begun to *greet* and *bow* to me. What is a greeting?—ah, how much it means to the faith of man!

You know my good manners and, therefore, will believe me when I say that I was cold and restrained like a gentleman who has just received a legacy. But if you had put your ear to my belly you would have heard violins playing within. Something about love, you understand. Oh, you understand everything. And thus, with these violins did I come to Magnus in the evening when the moon was shining brightly. Magnus was alone. We were long silent and this indicated that an interesting conversation awaited me. Finally I said:

"How is the Signorina's health?"…

But he interrupted me:

"We are facing a very difficult talk, Wondergood? Does that disturb you?"

"Oh, no, not at all."

"Do you want wine? Well, never mind. I shall drink a little but you need not. Yes, Wondergood?"

He laughed as he poured out the wine and here I noticed with astonishment that he himself was *very* excited: his large, white, hangman's hands were quite noticeably trembling. I do not know exactly just when my violins ceased—I think it was at that very moment. Magnus gulped down two glasses of wine—he had intended to take only a little—and, sitting down, continued:

"No, you ought not to drink, Wondergood. I need all your *senses*, undimmed by anything…you didn't drink anything to-day? No? That's good. Your *senses* must be clear and sober. One must not take anesthetics in such cases as…as…."

"As vivisection?"

He shook his head seriously in affirmation.

"Yes, vivisection. You have caught my idea marvelously. Yes, in cases of vivisection of the soul. For instance, when a loving mother is informed of the death of her son or…a rich man that he has become penniless. But the senses, what can we do with the senses, we cannot hold them in leash all our life! You understand, Wondergood? In the long run, I am not in the least so cruel a man as I occasionally seem even to myself and the *pain* of others frequently arouses in me an unpleasant, responsive trembling. That is not good. A surgeon's hand must be firm."

He looked at his fingers: they no longer trembled. He continued with a smile:

"However, wine helps some. Dear Wondergood, I swear by eternal salvation, by which you love so to swear, that it is extremely unpleasant for me to cause you this little…pain. Keep your senses, Wondergood! Your senses, your senses! Your hand, my friend?"

I gave him my hand and Magnus enveloped my palm and fingers and held them long in his own paw, strained, permeated with some kind of electric currents. Then he let them go, sighing with relief.

"That's it. Just so. Courage, Wondergood!"

I shrugged my shoulders, lit a cigar and asked:

"Your illustration of the *very* wealthy man who has suddenly become a beggar,—does that concern me? Am I penniless?"

Magnus answered slowly as he gazed straight into my eyes:

"If you wish to put it that way—yes. You have nothing left. Absolutely nothing. And this palace, too, is already sold. To-morrow the new owners take possession."

"Oh, that is interesting. And where are my billions?"

"I have them. They are mine. I am a very wealthy man, Wondergood."

I moved my cigar to the other corner of my mouth and asked:

"And you are ready, of course, to give me a helping hand? You are a contemptible scoundrel, Thomas Magnus."

"If that's what you call me—yes. Something on that order."

"And a liar!"

"Perhaps. In general, dear Wondergood, it is very necessary for you to change your outlook on life and man. You are too much of an idealist."

"And you"—I rose from my chair—"for you it is necessary to change your fellow conversationalist. Permit me to bid you good-by and to send a police commissary in my place."

Magnus laughed.

"Nonsense, Wondergood! Everything has been done within the law. You, yourself, have handed over everything to me. This will surprise no one…with your love for humanity. Of course, you can proclaim yourself insane. You understand?—and then, perhaps, I may get to the penitentiary. But you—you will land in an insane asylum. You would hardly like that, dear friend. Police! Well, go on talking. It will relieve the first effects of the blow."

I think it was really difficult for me to conceal my excitement. I hurled my cigar angrily into the fireplace, while my eye carefully measured both the window and Magnus…no, this carcass was too big to play ball with.

At that moment the loss of my wealth had not yet fully impressed itself upon my mind and it was that which maddened me as much as the brazen tone of Magnus and the patronizing manner of the old scoundrel. In addition, I dimly sensed something portentous of evil and sorrow, like a threat: as if some real danger were lurking not in front of me but behind my back.

"What is this all about?" I shouted, stamping my foot.

"What is this all about?" replied Magnus, like an echo. "Yes, I really cannot understand why you are so excited, Wondergood. You have so frequently offered me this money and even forced it upon me and now, when the money is in my hands, you want to call the police! Of course," Magnus smiled—"there is a slight distinction here: in placing your money so magnanimously at my *disposal*, you still remained its master and the master of the situation, while now…you understand, old friend: now I can simply drive you out of this house!"

I looked at Magnus significantly. He replied with no less a significant shrug of the shoulders and cried angrily:

"Stop your nonsense. I am stronger than you are. Do not try to be more of a fool than is absolutely necessitated by the situation."

"You are an unusually brazen scoundrel, Signor Magnus!"

"Again! How these sentimental souls do seek consolation in words! Take a cigar and listen to me. I have long needed money, a great deal of money. In my past, which I need not disclose to you, I have suffered certain…failures. They irritated me considerably. Fools and sentimental souls, you understand? My energy was imprisoned under lock and key, like a bird in a cage. For three years I sat in this cursed cage, awaiting my chance…."

"And all that—in the beautiful Campagna?"

"Yes, in the beautiful Campagna…and I had already begun to lose hope, when you appeared. I find it difficult to express myself at this point…."

"Be as direct as you can. Have no compunctions."

"You seemed very strange with all this love of yours for men and your *play*, as you finally termed it, and, my friend, for a long time I had grave doubts as to what you really were: an extraordinary fool or just a scoundrel, like myself. You see, such extraordinary asses appear so seldom that even I had my doubts. You are not angry?"

"Oh, not at all."

"You forced money upon me and I thought: a trap! However you made your moves quickly and certain precautions on my part…."

"Pardon me for interrupting. So, those books of yours, your solitary contemplation of life, that little white house and everything was all a lie? And murder—do you remember all that drivel about hands steeped in blood?"

"Yes, I did kill. That is true. And I have pondered much upon life, while awaiting you, but the rest, of course, was falsehood. Very base falsehood, but you were so credulous…."

"And.. Maria?"

I confess that I had hardly uttered this name when I felt something clutching at my throat. Magnus looked at me sharply and said gloomily:

"We will discuss Maria, too. But how excited you are! Even your nails have turned blue. Perhaps you'll have some wine? Well, never mind. Have patience. I shall continue. When you began your affair with Maria…of course with my slight assistance…I finally concluded that you were…."

"An extraordinary ass?"

Magnus raised his hand in a consoling gesture:

"Oh, no! You seemed to me to be that at the beginning. I will tell you quite truthfully, as I do everything I am telling you now: you are not a fool at all, Wondergood. I have grown to know you more intimately. It doesn't matter that you have so naïvely surrendered your billions to me…many wise men have been fooled before by clever…scoundrels! Your misfortune is quite another thing."

I had the strength to smile:

"My love for human beings?"

"No, my friend: your contempt for human beings! Your *contempt* and at the same time your naïve faith in them arising from it. You regard human beings so far below you, you are so convinced of their fatal powerlessness that you do not fear them at all and are quite ready to pat the rattlesnake's head: such a nice little rattlesnake! One should fear people, comrade! I know your *game*, but at times you were quite sincere in your prattle about man, you even pitied him, but from an elevation or from a sidetrack—I know not which. Oh, if you could only hate people I would take you along with me with pleasure. But you are an egotist, a terrible egotist, Wondergood, and I am even beginning to shed my regrets for having robbed you, when I think of that! Whence comes this base contempt of yours?"

"I am still only learning to be a man."

"Well, go on learning. But why do you call your professor a scoundrel: For I am your professor, Wondergood!"

"To the devil with this prattle. So…you do not intend to take me along with you?"

"No, my friend, I do not."

"So. Only my billions. Very well, but what about your plan: to blow up the earth or something of that kind? Or did you lie on this point, too? I cannot believe that you simply intend to open…a money changer's bureau or become some ragged king!"

Magnus looked at me gloomily. There was even a gleam of sympathy in his eyes as he replied slowly:

"No, on that point I did not lie. But you won't do for me. You would always be hanging on to my coat tails. Just now you shouted: liar, scoundrel, thief…. It's strange, but you are yet only learning to be a man and you have already imbibed so much pettiness. When I shall raise my hand to strike some one, your contempt will begin to whine: don't strike, leave him alone, have pity. Oh, if you could only hate! No, you are a terrible egotist, old man."

I shouted:

"The devil take you with your harping on this egotism! I am not in the least more stupid than you, you beast, and I cannot understand what you find so saintly in hatred!"

Magnus frowned:

"First of all: don't shout or I'll throw you out. Do you hear? Yes, perhaps you are no more stupid than I am, but man's business is not your business. Do you realize that, you beast? In blowing up things, I only intend to do business and you want to be the ruler of another's plant. Let them steal and break down the machinery and you—you will be concerned only about your salary and the respect due you? And I—I won't stand that! All this,"—he swept the room with a broad gesture—"is my plant, *mine*, do you hear, and it is I who will be robbed. I will be robbed and injured. And I hate those who rob me. What would you have done, in the long run, with your billions, if I had not taken them from you? Built conservatories and raised heirs—for the perpetuation of your kind? Private yachts and diamonds for your wife? And I…give me all the gold on earth and I will throw it all into the flames of my hatred. And all because I have been insulted! When you see a hunchback you throw him a lire. So that he may continue to bear his hump, yes? And I want to destroy him, to kill him, to burn him like a crooked log. To whom do you appeal when you are fooled or when a dog bites your finger? To your wife, the police, public opinion? But suppose the wife, with the aid of your butler, plants horns on your head or public opinion fails to understand you and instead of pitying you prefers to give you a thrashing—then do you make your appeal to God? But I, I go to no one. I plead before no one, but neither do I forgive. You understand? I do not forgive! Only egotists forgive! I consider myself personally insulted!"

I heard him in silence. Perhaps it was because I was so close to the fireplace, gazing into the fire and listening to Magnus's words, each new word intermingled with a fresh blaze of a burning log; no sooner would the glowing red mass fall apart than the words, too, would break up into particles, like hot coals. My head was not at all clear and, under the influence of these burning, flaming, flying words I fell into a strange, dark drowsiness. But this was what my memory retained:

"Oh, if you could only hate! If you were not so cowardly and weak of soul! I would take you with me and would let you behold a fire which would forever dry your miserable tears and burn your sentimental dreams to ashes! Do you hear the song of the fools of the world? They are merely loading the cannons. The wise man need only apply the fire to the fuse, you understand? Could you behold calmly the sight of a blissful sheep and hungry snake lying together, separated only by a thin partition? I could not! I would drill just a little opening, a little opening…the rest they would do themselves. Do you know that from the union of truth and falsehood comes an explosion? I want to unite. I shall do nothing myself: I shall only *complete* what they have begun. Do you hear how merrily they sing? I will make them dance, too! Come with me, comrade! You sought some sort of a play—let me give you an extraordinary spectacle! We shall bring the whole earth into action and millions of marionettes will begin to caper obediently at our command: you know not yet how talented and obliging they are. It will be a splendid play and will give you much pleasure and amusement…."

A large log fell apart and split into many sparks and hot cinders. The flame subsided, growing morose and red. A silent heat emanated from the dimmed, smoke-smeared hearth. It burned my face and suddenly there arose before me my puppets' show. The heat and fire had conjured up a mirage. I seemed to hear the crash of drums and the gay ring of cymbals, while the merry clown turned on his head at the sight of the broken skulls of the dolls. The broken heads continued to pile up. Then I saw the scrap heap, with two motionless little legs protruding from the heap of rubbish. They wore rose slippers. And the drums continued beating: tump-tump-tump. And I said pensively:

"I think it will hurt them."

And behind my back rang out the contemptuous and indifferent reply:

"Quite possibly."

"Tump-tump-tump…."

"It is all the same to you, Wondergood, but I cannot! Can't you see: I cannot permit every miserable biped to call himself a man. There are too many of them, already. They multiply like rabbits, under the stimulus of physicians and laws. Death, deceived, cannot handle them all. It is confused and seems to have lost its dignity and moral authority. It is wasting its time in dancing halls. I hate them. It has become repulsive to me to walk upon this earth, fallen into the power of a strange, strange species. We must suspend the law, at least temporarily, and let death have its fling. However, they themselves will see to this. No, not I, but they, will do it. Think not that I am particularly cruel, no—I am only logical. I am only the conclusion, the symbol of equality, the sum total, the line beneath the column of figures. You may call it Ergo, Magnus, Ergo! They say: 'two and two' and I reply: 'four.' Exactly four. Imagine that the world has suddenly grown cold and immovable for a moment and you behold some such picture: here is a free and careless head and above it—a suspended axe. Here is a mass of powder and here a spark about to fall upon it. But it has stopped and does not fall. Here is a heavy structure, set upon a single, undermined foundation. But everything has grown rigid and the foundation holds. Here is a breast and here a hand aiming a bullet at it. Have I prepared all this? I merely touch the lever and press it down. The axe falls upon the laughing head and crushes it. The spark falls into the powder—all is off! The building crashes to the ground. The bullet pierces the ready breast. And I—I have merely touched the lever, I, Magnus Ergo! Think: would I be able to kill had I at my disposal only violins or other musical instruments?"

I laughed:

"Only violins!"

Magnus replied with laughter: his voice was hoarse and heavy:

"But they have other instruments, too! And I will use these instruments. See how simple and interesting all this is?"

"And what further, Magnus Ergo?"

"How do I know what's to follow? I see only *this* page and solve only *this* problem. I know not what the next page contains."

"Perhaps it contains the same thing?"

"Perhaps it does. And perhaps this is the final page…well, what of that: the sum total remains as is necessary."

"You spoke on one occasion about *miracles*?"

"Yes, that is my lever. You remember what I told you *about my* explosive? I promise rabbits to make lions of them…. You see, a rabbit cannot stand brains. Give a rabbit brains and he will hang himself. Melancholy will drive him to suicide. Brains implies logic and what can *logic* promise to a rabbit? Nothing but a sorry fate on a restaurant menu. What one must promise a rabbit is either immortality for a cheap price, as does Cardinal X. or—heaven on earth. You will see what energy, what daring, etc., my rabbit will develop when I paint before him on the wall heavenly powers and gardens of Eden!"

"On the wall?"

"Yes,—on a stone wall. He will storm it with all the power of his species! And who knows…who knows…perhaps this mass may really break through this stone wall?"

Magnus lapsed into thought. I drew away from the now extinguished fire and looked upon the explosive head of my repulsive friend…. Something naïve, like two little wrinkles, almost like those of a child, lay upon his stony brow. I burst into laughter and shouted:

"Thomas Magnus! Thomas Ergo! Do you believe?"

Without raising his head, as if he had not heard my laughter, he lifted his eyes and replied pensively:

"We must try."

But I continued to laugh: deep, wild—apparently human—laughing malice began to rise within me:

"Thomas Magnus! Magnus Rabbit! Do you believe?"

He thumped the table with his fist and roared in a wild transport:

"Be quiet! I tell you: we must try. How do I know? I have never yet been on Mars nor seen this earth inside-out. Be silent, accursed egotist! You know nothing of our affairs. Ah, if only you could hate!…"

"I hate already."

Magnus suddenly laughed and grew strangely calm. He sat down and scrutinizing me from all possible angles, as if he did not believe me, he burst out:

"You? Hate? Whom?"

"You."

He looked me over as carefully again and shook his head in doubt:

"Is that true, Wondergood?"

"If they are rabbits, you are the most repulsive of them all, because you are a mixture of rabbit and…Satan. You are a coward! The fact that you are a crook, a thief, a liar, a murderer is not important. But you are a coward! That is important. I expected something more of you. I hoped your mind would lift you above the greatest crime, but you lift crime itself into some base philanthropy. You are as much of a lackey as the others. The only difference between you and them is that you have a perverted idea of service!"

Magnus sighed.

"No, that's not it. You understand nothing, Wondergood."

"And what you lack is daring, my friend. If you are Magnus Ergo… what audacity: Magnus Ergo!—then why don't you go the limit? Then, I, too, would follow you…perhaps!"

"Will you really come?"

"And why should I not come? Let me be Contempt, and you— Hatred. We can go together. Do not fear lest I hang on to your coat tails. You have revealed much to me, my dear putridity, and I shall not seize your hand even though you raise it against yourself."

"Will you betray me?"

"And you will kill me. Is that not enough?"

But Magnus shook his head doubtfully and said:

"You will betray me. I am a living human being, while you smell like a corpse. I do not want to have contempt for *myself*. If I do, I perish. Don't you dare to look at me! Look upon the others!"

I laughed.

"Very well. I shall not look at *you*. I will look at the rest. I will make it easier for you with my contempt."

Magnus fell into prolonged thought. Then he looked again at me piercingly and quietly asked:

"And Maria?…"

Oh, cursed wretch! Again he hurled my heart upon the floor! I looked at him wildly, like one aroused at night by fire. And three big waves swept my breast. With the first wave rose the silent violins…ah, how they wailed, just as if the musician played not upon strings but upon my veins! Then in a huge wave with foamy surf there rolled by all the images, thoughts and emotions of my recent, beloved human state: think of it: everything was there! Even the lizzard that hissed at my feet that evening beneath the moonlight. I recalled even the little lizzard! And with the third wave there was rolled out quietly upon the shore the holy name: *Maria*. And just as quietly it receded, leaving behind a delicate lace of foam, and from beyond the sea burst forth the rays of the sun, and for a moment, for one, little moment, I again became a white schooner, with sails lowered. Where were the stars while awaiting the word of the Lord of the universe to break forth in all their brilliance? Madonna!

Magnus recalled me quietly.

"Where are you going? She is not there. What do you want?"

"Pardon me, dear Magnus, but I would like to see the Signorina Maria. Only for a moment. I don't feel quite well. There is something revolving in my eyes and head. Are you smiling, dear Magnus, or does it only seem so to me? I have been gazing into the fire too long and I can hardly discern the objects before me. Did you say: Maria? Yes, I would like to see her. Then we shall continue our interesting conversation. You will remind me just where we stopped, but meanwhile I would be extremely obliged to you, if we were…to take a little drive into the Campagna. It is so sweet there. And Signorina Maria…."

"Sit down. You will see her presently."

But I continued to weave my nonsense—what in the devil had happened to my head! I prattled on for a considerable period and now the whole thing seems so ridiculous: Once or twice I pressed the heavy, motionless hand of Thomas Magnus: apparently he must have looked like my father at that moment. Finally, I subsided, partially regained my senses but, in obedience to Magnus' command, remained in my chair and prepared to listen.

"Can you listen now? You are quite excited, old man. Remember: the senses, the Senses!"

"Yes, now I can go on. I…remember everything. Continue, old friend. I am all attention."

Yes, I recollected everything but it was quite immaterial to me just what Magnus said or what he might say: I was awaiting Maria. That is how strong my love was! Turning aside for some reason and beating time with his fingers on the table, Magnus said slowly and rather reluctantly:

"Listen, Wondergood. In reality, it would be much more convenient for me to throw you out into the street, you and your idiotic Toppi. You wanted to experience *all* human life and I would have viewed with pleasure any efforts on your part to earn your own bread. You are apparently no longer used to this? It would also have been very interesting to know what would become of your grandiose contempt when…. But I am not angry. Strange to say, I even nurse a feeling of thankfulness for your…billions. And I am rather hopeful. Yes, I still have a little hope that some day you may really grow to be a man. And while this may prove an impediment to me, I am ready to take you with me, but only—after a certain test. Are you still anxious to have…Maria?"

"Yes."

"Very well."

Magnus rose with effort and moved toward the door. But he halted for a moment and turned toward me and—surprising as it was on the part of this scoundrel—he kissed my brow.

"Sit down, old man. I will call her immediately. The servants are all out to-day."

He uttered the last sentence as he knocked feebly at the door. The head of one of his *aides* appeared for a moment and immediately withdrew. With apparently the same effort Magnus returned to his place and said with a sigh:

"She will be here at once."

We were silent. I fixed my eyes upon the tall door and it opened wide. *Maria* entered. With a quick step I moved to greet her and bowed low. Magnus shouted:

"Don't kiss that hand!"

May 27.

I could not continue these notes yesterday. Do not laugh! This mere combination of words: do not kiss that hand!—seemed to me the most terrible utterance the human tongue was capable of. It acted upon me like a magic curse. When I recall those words now they *interrupt* everything I do and befog my whole being, transporting me into a new state. If I happen to be speaking I grow silent, as if suddenly stricken dumb. If I happen to be walking, I halt. If standing, I run. If I happen to be asleep, no matter how deep my slumber, I awake and cannot fall asleep again. Very simple, extremely simple words: Do not kiss that hand!

And now listen to what happened further:

And so: I bowed over *Maria's* hand. But so strange and sudden was Magnus' cry, so great was the command in his hoarse voice, that it was impossible to disobey. It was as if he had stopped a blind man on the edge of a precipice! *But* I failed to grasp his meaning and raised my head in perplexity, still holding Maria's hand in mine, and looked at Magnus. He was breathing heavily, as if he had actually witnessed my fall into the abyss—and in reply to my questioning look, he said in a stifled tone:

"Let her hand alone. Maria get away from him."

Maria released her hand and stepped aside, at a distance from me. Still perplexed I watched her, standing alone! I tried to grasp the situation. For a brief moment it seemed even extremely ludicrous and reminded me of a scene in a comedy, in which the angry father comes unexpectedly upon the sweethearts, but my silly laughter died away immediately and in obedient expectation I raised my eyes to Magnus.

Magnus hesitated. Rising with an effort, he twice paced the length of the room and halting before me, with his hands clasped behind him, said:

"With all your eccentricities, you're a decent man, Wondergood. I have *robbed* you (that was how he put it) but I can no longer permit you to kiss the hand of this woman. Listen! Listen! I have already told you you must change your outlook upon men. I know it is very difficult and I sympathize with you, but it is essential that you do it, old friend. Listen! Listen! I misled you: Maria is not my daughter…I have no children. Neither is she a…Madonna. She is my mistress and she was that as recently as last night.…"

Now I understand that Magnus was merciful in his own way and was intentionally submerging me slowly into darkness. But at that time I did not realize this and *slowly* stifling, my breath gradually dying, I lost consciousness. And when with Magnus' last words the light fled from me and impenetrable night enveloped my being, I whipped out my revolver and fired at Magnus several times in succession. I do not know how many shots I fired. I remember only a series of laughing, flickering flames and the movements of my hand, pushing the weapon forward. I cannot remember at all how and when his *aides* rushed in and disarmed me. When I regained my senses this was the picture I saw: the *aides* were gone. I was sitting deep in my chair before the dark fireplace, my hair was wet, while above my left eyebrow there was a bandage soaked in blood. My collar was gone and my shirt was torn, my left sleeve was almost entirely torn off, so that I had to keep jerking it up constantly. Maria stood on the same spot, in the same pose, as if she had not moved at all during the struggle. I was surprised to see Toppi, who sat in a corner and gazed at me strangely. At the table, with his back to me, stood Magnus. He was pouring out some wine for himself.

When I heaved a particularly deep sigh, Magnus turned quickly and said in a strangely familiar tone:

"Do you want some wine, Wondergood? You may have a glass now. Here, drink.… You see you failed to hit me. I do not know whether to be glad or not, but I am alive. To your health, old man!"

I touched my brow with my finger and mumbled:

"Blood.…"

"A mere trifle, just a little scratch. It won't matter. Don't touch it."

"It smells."

"With powder? Yes, that'll soon pass, too. Toppi is here. Do you see him? He asked permission to stay here. You won't object if your secretary remains while we continue our conversation? He is extremely devoted to you."

I looked at Toppi and smiled. Toppi made a grimace and sighed gently:

"Mr. Wondergood! It is I, your Toppi."

And he burst into tears. This old devil, still emitting the odor of fur, this old clown in black, this sexton with hanging nose, this seducer of little girls—burst into tears! But still worse was it when, blinking my eyes, I, too, began to weep, I, "the wise, immortal, almighty!" Thus we both wept, two deceived devils who happened to drop in upon this earth, and human beings—I am happy to give them their due!—looked on with deep sympathy for our tears. Weeping and laughing at the same time, I asked:

"It's difficult to be a man, Toppi?"

And Toppi, sobbing, replied obediently:

"Very difficult, Mr. Wondergood."

But here I happened to look at Maria and my sentimental tears immediately dried. In general, that evening is memorable for the sudden and ludicrous transformations of my moods. You probably know them, old man? Now I wept and beat the lyre, like a weeping post, now I became permeated with a stony calm and a sense of unconquerable power, or I began to chatter nonsense, like a parrot scared to death by a dog, and kept up my chatter, louder, sillier and more and more unbearable, until a new mood bore me off into a deep and inexpressible sadness. Magnus caught my look at Maria and smiled involuntarily. I adjusted the collar of my torn shirt and said *dryly*:

"I do not know whether to be glad or sorry that I failed to kill you, old friend. I am quite calm now, however, and would like you to tell me everything about…that woman. But as you are a liar, let me question her first. Signorina Maria, you were my bride? And in a few days I hoped to call you my wife. But tell me the truth: are you really…this man's mistress?"

"Yes, signor."

"And…how long?"

"Five years, signor."

"And how old are you now."

"Nineteen, signor."

"That means you were fourteen…. Now you may continue, Magnus."

"Oh, my God!"

(It was Toppi who exclaimed.)

"Sit down, Maria.—As you see, Wondergood,"—began Magnus in a dry and calm tone, as if he were demonstrating not himself but some sort of a chemical compound—"this mistress of mine is quite an extraordinary phenomenon. With all her unusual resemblance to the Madonna, capable of deceiving men better versed than you or I in religion, with all her really unearthly beauty, chastity and charm—she is a licentious and quite shameless creature, ready to sell herself from head to foot...."

"Magnus!"

"Calm yourself. You see how she listens to me? Even your old Toppi is cringing and blushing while she—her gaze is clear and all her features are filled with placid harmony...did you notice how clear Maria's gaze is? Do you hear me?"

"Yes, certainly."

"Would you like wine or an orange? Take it. There it is on the table. Incidentally, observe her graceful walk: she seems to be always stepping lightly as if on flowers or clouds. What extraordinary beauty and litheness! As an old lover of hers, I may also add the following detail which you have not learned yet: she herself, her body, has the fragrance of some flowers. Now as to her spiritual qualities, as the psychologists put it. If I were to speak of them in ordinary language, I would say she was as stupid as a goose,—quite a hopeless fool. But she is cunning. And a liar. Very avaricious as regards money but she likes it only in gold. Everything she told you she learned from me, memorizing the more difficult lines...and I had quite a task in teaching her. But I feared all the time that, despite your love, you would be struck by her apparent lack of brains and that is why I kept her from you the last few days."

Toppi sobbed:

"Oh, God! Madonna!"

"Does this astonish you, Mr. Toppi?"—Magnus asked, turning his head. "I dare say you are not alone. Do you remember, Wondergood, what I told you about Maria's *fatal* resemblance, which drove one young man to suicide. I did not lie to you altogether: the youth actually did kill himself when he realized who Maria really was. He was pure of soul. He loved as you do and as you he could not bear—how do you put it?—the wreck of his ideal."

Magnus laughed:

"Do you remember Giovanni, Maria?"

"Slightly."

"Do you hear, Wondergood?" asked Magnus, laughing. "That is exactly the tone in which she would have spoken of me a week hence if you had killed me to-day. Have another orange, Maria.... But if I were to speak of Maria in extraordinary language—she is not at all stupid. She simply doesn't happen to have what is called a soul. I have frequently tried to look deep into her heart and thoughts and I have always ended in vertigo, as if I had been hurled to the edge of an abyss: there was *nothing* there. Emptiness. You have probably observed, Wondergood, or you, Mr. Toppi, that ice is not as cold as the brow of a *dead* man? And no matter what emptiness familiar to you you may imagine, my friends, it cannot be compared with that absolute vacuum which forms the kernel of my beautiful, light-giving star. Star of the Seas?—that was what you once called her, Wondergood, was it not?"

Magnus laughed again and gulped down a glass of wine. He drank a great deal that evening.

"Will you have some wine, Mr. Toppi? No? Well, suit yourself. I'll take some. So that is why, Mr. Wondergood, I did not want you to kiss the hand of that creature. Don't turn your eyes away, old friend. Imagine you are in a museum and look straight at her, bravely. Did you wish to say something, Toppi?"

"Yes, Signor Magnus. Pardon me, Mr. Wondergood, but I would like to ask your permission to leave. As a gentleman, although not much of that, I…cannot remain…at…."

Magnus narrowed his eyes derisively:

"At such a scene?"

"Yes, at such a scene, when one gentleman, with the silent approval of another gentleman, insults a woman like *that*," exclaimed Toppi, extremely irritated, and rose. Magnus, just as ironically, turned to me:

"And what do you say, Wondergood? Shall we release this little, extremely little, gentleman?"

"Stay, Toppi."

Toppi sat down obediently.

From the moment Magnus resumed, I, for the first time, regained my breath and looked at Maria.

What shall I say to you? It was *Maria*. And here I understood a little *what* happens in one's brain when one begins to go mad.

"May I continue?" asked Magnus. "However, I have little to add. Yes, I took her when she was fourteen or fifteen years old. She herself does not know how old she really is, but I was not her first lover…nor the tenth. I could never learn her past exactly. She either lies cunningly or is actually devoid of memory. But even the most subtle questioning, which even a most expert criminal could not dodge, neither bribes nor gifts, nor threats—and she is extremely cowardly!—could compel her to reveal herself. She does not 'remember.' That's all. But her deep licentiousness, enough to shame the Sultan himself, her extraordinary experience and daring in ars amandi confirms my suspicion that she received her training in a lupanaria or…or at the court of some Nero. I do not know how old she is and she seems to change constantly. Why should I not say that she is 20 or 2000 years old? Maria…you can do everything and you know everything?"

I did not look at that woman. But in her answer there was a slight displeasure:

"Don't talk nonsense. What will Mr. Wondergood think of me?"

Magnus broke into loud laughter and struck the table with his glass:

"Do you hear, Wondergood? She covets your good opinion. And if I should command her to undress at once in your presence…."

"Oh, my God! My God!"—sobbed Toppi and covered his face with his hands. I glanced quickly into Magnus' eyes—and remained rigid in the terrible enchantment of his gaze. His face was laughing. This pale mask of his was still lined with traces of faint laughter but the eyes were dim and inscrutable. Directed upon me, they stared off somewhere into the distance and were horrible in their expression of dark and *empty* madness: only the empty orbits of a skull could gaze so threateningly and in such wrath.

And again darkness filled my head and when I regained my senses Magnus had already turned and calmly sipped his wine. Without changing his position, he raised his glass to the light, smelled the wine, sipped some more of it and said as calmly as before:

"And so, Wondergood, my friend. Now you know about all there is to know of Maria or the Madonna, as you called her, and I ask you: will you take her or not? I give her away. Take her. If you say yes, she will be in your bedroom to-day and…I swear by eternal salvation, you will pass a very pleasant night. Well, what do you say?"

"Yesterday, you, and to-day, I?"

"Yesterday I,—to-day, you." He smiled: "What kind of man are you, Wondergood, to speak of such trifles. Or aren't you used to having some one else warm your bed? Take her. She is a fine girl."

"Whom are you torturing, Magnus:—me or yourself?"

Magnus looked at me ironically:

"What a wise boy! Of course, myself! You are a very clever American, Mr. Wondergood, and I wonder why your career has been so mediocre. Go to bed, dear children. Good night. What are you looking at, Wondergood: do you find the hour too early? If so, take her out for a walk in the garden. When you see Maria beneath the moonlight, 3000 Magnuses will be unable to prove that this heavenly maiden is the same creature who…."

I flared up:

"You are a disgusting scoundrel and liar, Thomas Magnus! If she has received her training in a lupanaria, then you, my worthy signor, must have received your higher education in the penitentiary. Whence comes that aroma which permeates so thoroughly your gentlemanly jokes and witticisms. The sight of your pale face is beginning to nauseate me. After enticing a woman in the fashion of a petty, common hero...."

Magnus struck the table with his fist. His bloodshot eyes were aflame.

"Silence! You are an inconceivable ass, Wondergood! Don't you understand that I myself, like you, was deceived by her? Who, meeting *Madonna*, can escape deception? Oh devil! What are the sufferings of your little, shallow American soul in comparison with the pangs of mine? Oh devil! Witticism, jests, gentlemen and ladies, asses and tigers, gods and devils! Can't you see: this is not a woman, this is—an eagle who daily plucks my liver! My suffering begins in the morning. Each morning, oblivious to what passed the day before, I see Madonna before me and believe. I think: what happened to me yesterday? Apparently, I must be mistaken or did I miss anything? It is impossible that this clear gaze, this divine walk, this pure countenance of Madonna should belong to a prostitute. It is your soul that is vile, Thomas Magnus: she is as pure as a host. And there were occasions when, on my knees, I actually begged forgiveness of this creature! Can you imagine it: on my knees! Then it was that I was really a scoundrel, Wondergood. I idealized her, endowed her with my thoughts and feelings and was overjoyed, like an idiot. I almost wept with felicity when she mumblingly repeated what I would say. Like a high priest I painted my idol and then knelt before it in intoxication! But the truth proved stronger at last. With each moment, with each hour, falsehood slipped off her body, so that, toward night, I even beat her. I beat her and wept. I beat her cruelly as does a procurer his mistress. And then came night with its Babylonian licentiousness, the sleep of the dead and—oblivion. And then morning again. And again Madonna. And again...oh, devil! Over night my faith again grew, as did the liver of Prometheus, and like a bird of prey she tortured me all day. I, too, am human, Wondergood!"

Shivering as if with cold, Magnus began to pace the room rapidly, gazed into the dark fireplace and approached Maria. Maria lifted her clear gaze to him, as if in question, while Magnus stroked her head carefully and gently, as he would that of a parrot or a cat:

"What a little head! What a sweet, little head.... Wondergood! Come, caress it!"

I drew up my torn sleeve and asked ironically:

"And it is this bird of prey that you now wish to give to me? Have you exhausted your feed? You want my liver, too, in addition to my billions?"

But Magnus had already calmed himself. Subduing his excitement and the drunkenness which had imperceptibly come upon him, he returned to his place without haste and ordered politely:

"I will answer you in a moment, Mr. Wondergood. Please withdraw to your room Maria. I have something to say to Mr. Wondergood. And I would ask you, too, my honorable Mr. Toppi, to depart. You may join my friends in the salon."

"If Mr. Wondergood will so command...." replied Toppi, dryly, without rising.

I nodded and, without looking at Magnus, my secretary obediently made his exit. Maria, too, left the room. To tell the truth, I again felt like clinging to his vest and weeping in the first few moments of my tête-à-tête with Magnus: after all, this thief was my friend! But I satisfied myself with merely swallowing my tears. Then followed a moment of brief desperation at the *departure* of Maria. And slowly, as if from the realm of remote recollection, blind and wild anger and the need of beating and destroying began to fill my heart. Let me add, too, that I was extremely provoked by my torn sleeve that kept slipping constantly: it was necessary for me to be stern and austere and this made me seem ridiculous... ah, on what trifles does the result of the greatest events depend on this earth! I lighted a cigar and with studied gruffness hurled into the calm and hateful face of Magnus:

"Now, you! Enough of comedy and charlatanism. Tell me what you want. So you want me to surrender to that bird of prey of yours?"

Magnus replied calmly, although his eyes were burning with anger:

"Yes. That is the trial I wanted to subject you to, Wondergood. I fear that I have succumbed slightly to the emotion of useless and vain revenge and spoke more heatedly than was necessary in Maria's presence. The thing is, Wondergood, that all that I have so picturesquely described to you, all this passion and despair and all these sufferings of...Prometheus really belong to the past. I now look upon Maria without pain and even with a certain amount of pleasure, as upon a beautiful and useful little beast...useful for domestic considerations. You understand? What after all, is the liver of Prometheus? It is all nonsense! In reality, I should be thankful to Maria. She gnawed out with her little teeth my silly *faith* and gave me that clear, firm and realistic outlook upon life which permits of no deceptions and...sentimentalisms. You, too, ought to experience and grasp it, Wondergood, if you would follow Magnus Ergo."

I remained silent, lazily chewing my cigar. Magnus lowered his eyes and continued still more calmly and dryly:

"Desert pilgrims, to accustom themselves to death, used to sleep in coffins: let Maria be your coffin and when you feel like going to church, kissing a woman and stretching your hand to a friend, just look at Maria and her *father*, Thomas Magnus. Take her, Wondergood, and you will soon convince yourself of the value of my gift. I don't need her any longer. And when your humiliated soul shall become inflamed with truly inextinguishable, human hatred and not with weak contempt, come to me and I shall welcome you into the ranks of my yeomanry, which will very soon…. Are you hesitating? Well, then go, catch other lies, but be careful to avoid scoundrels and Madonnas, my gentleman from Illinois!"

He broke into loud laughter and swallowed a glass of wine at one gulp. His swollen calm evaporated. Little flames of intoxication, now merry, now ludicrous, like the lights of a carnival, now triumphant, now dim, like funeral torches at a grave, again sprang forth in his bloodshot eyes. The scoundrel was drunk but held himself firmly, merely swaying his branches, like an oak before a south wind. Rising and facing me, he straightened his body cynically, as if trying to reveal himself in his entirety, and well nigh spat these words at me:

"Well? How long do you intend to think about it, you ass? Come, quick, or I'll kick you out! Quick! I'm tired of you! What's the use of my wasting words? What are you thinking of?"

My head buzzed. Madly pulling up that accursed sleeve of mine, I replied:

"I am thinking that you are an evil, contemptible, stupid and repulsive beast! I am thinking in what springs of life or hell itself I could find for you the punishment you deserve! Yes, I came upon this earth to play and to laugh. Yes, I myself was ready to embrace any evil. I myself lied and pretended, but you, hairy worm, you crawled into my very heart and bit me. You took advantage of the fact that my heart was human and bit me, you hairy worm. How dared you deceive me? I will punish you."

"You? Me?"

I am glad to say that Magnus was astonished and taken aback. His eyes widened and grew round and his open mouth naïvely displayed a set of white teeth. Breathing with difficulty, he repeated:

"You? Me?"

"Yes. I—you."

"Police?"

"You are not afraid of it? Very well. Let all your courts be powerless, remain unpunished on this earth, you evil conscienceless creature! The day will come when the sea of falsehood, which constitutes your life, will part and all your falsehood, too, will give way and disappear. Let there be no foot upon this earth to crush you, hairy worm. Let! I, too, am powerless here. But the day will come when you will depart from this earth. And when you come to *Me* and fall under the shadow of my kingdom...."

"Your kingdom? Hold on, Wondergood. Who are you, then?"

And right at this point there occurred the most shameful event of my entire earthly life. Tell me: is it not ridiculously funny when Satan, even in human form, bends his knee in prayer to a prostitute and is stripped naked by the very first man he meets? Yes, this is extremely ridiculous and shameful of Satan, who bears with him the breath of eternity. But what would you say of Satan when he turned into a powerless and pitiful liar and pasted upon his head with a great flourish the paper crown of a theatrical czar? I am ashamed, old man. Give me one of your blows, the kind on which you feed your friends and hired clowns. Or has this torn sleeve brought me to this senseless, pitiful wrath? Or was this the last act of my human masquerade, when man's spirit descends to the mire and sweeps the dust and dirt with its breath? Or has the *ruin* of Madonna, which I witnessed, dragged Satan, too, into the same abyss?

But this was—think of it!—this was what I answered Magnus. Thrusting out my chest, barely covered with my torn shirt, stealthily pulling up my sleeve, so that it might not slip off entirely, and looking sternly and angrily directly into the stupid, and as they seemed to me, frightened eyes of the scoundrel Magnus, I replied *triumphantly*:

"I am—Satan!"

Magnus was silent for a moment—and then broke out into all the laughter that a drunken, repulsive, human belly can contain. Of course you, old man, expected that, but I did not. I swear by eternal salvation, I did not! I shouted something but the brazen laughter of this beast drowned my voice. Finally, taking advantage of a moment's interval between his thundering peals of laughter, I exclaimed quickly and modestly...like a footnote at the bottom of a page, like a commentary of a publisher:

"Don't you understand: I am Satan. I have donned the human form! I have donned the human form!"

He heard me with his eyes bulging, and with fresh thunderous roars of laughter, the outbursts shaking his entire frame, he moved toward the door, flung it open and shouted:

"Here! Come here! Here is Satan! In human...human garb!"

And he disappeared behind the door.

Oh, if I could only have fallen through the floor, disappeared or flown away, like a real devil, on wings, in that endless moment, during which he was gathering the *public* for an extraordinary spectacle. And now they came—all of them, damn them: Maria and all the six *aides* and my miserable Toppi, and Magnus himself, and completing the procession—His Eminence, Cardinal X.! The cursed, shaven monkey walked with great dignity and even bowed to me, after which he sat down, just as dignified, in an armchair and carefully covered his knees with his robes. All were wondering, not knowing yet what it was all about, and glanced now at me and now at Magnus, who tried hard to look serious.

"What's the trouble, Signor Magnus?" asked the Cardinal in a benevolent tone.

"Permit me to report the following, your Eminence: Mr. Henry Wondergood has just informed me that he is—Satan. Yes, Satan, and that he has merely donned the human form. And thus our assumption that he is an American from Illinois falls. Mr. Wondergood is Satan and apparently has but recently deigned to arrive from Hell. What shall we do about it, Your Eminence?"

Silence might have saved me. But how could I restrain this maddened Wondergood, whose heart was aflame with insult! Like a lackey who has appropriated his celebrated master's name and who faintly senses something of his grandeur, power and connections—Wondergood stepped forward and said with an ironic bow:

"Yes, I am Satan. But I must add to the speech of Signor Magnus that not only do I wear the human form but also that I have been robbed. Are those *two* scoundrels who have robbed me known to you, Your Eminence? And are you, perhaps, one of them, Your Eminence?"

Magnus alone continued to smile. The rest, it seemed to me, grew serious and awaited the Cardinal's reply. It followed. The shaven monkey, it developed, was not a bad actor. Pretending to be startled, the Cardinal raised his right hand and said with an expression of extreme goodness, contrasting sharply with his words and gesture:

"Vade Petro Satanas!"

I am not going to describe to you how they laughed. You can imagine it. Even Maria's teeth parted slightly. Almost losing consciousness from anger and impotence, I turned to Toppi for sympathy and aid. But Toppi, covering his face with his hands, was cringing in the corner, silent. Amid general laughter, and ringing far above it, came the heavy voice of Magnus, laden with infinite ridicule:

"Look at the plucked rooster. That is Satan!"

And again there came an outburst of laughter. His Eminence continuously shook, as though flapping his wings, and choked and whined. The monkey's gullet could hardly pass the cascades of laughter. I tore off that accursed sleeve madly and waving it like a flag, I ventured into a sea of falsehood, with full sails set. I knew that somewhere ahead there were rocks against which I might be shattered but the tempest of impotence and anger bore me on like a chip of wood.

I am ashamed to repeat my speech here. Every word of it was trembling and wailing with impotency. Like a village vicar, frightening his ignorant parishioners, I threatened them with *Hell* and with all the Dantean tortures of literary fame. Oh, I did know something that I might really have frightened them with but how could I express the *extraordinary* which is inexpressible in their language? And so I prattled on of eternal fire. Of eternal torture. Of unquenchable thirst. Of the gnashing of teeth. Of the fruitlessness of tears and pleading. And what else? Ah, even of red hot forks I prattled, maddened more and more by the indifference and shamelessness of these shallow faces, these small eyes, these mediocre souls, regarding themselves above punishment. But they remained unmoved and smug, as if in a fortress, beyond the walls of their mediocrity and fatal blindness. And all my words were shattered against their impenetrable skulls! And think of it, the only one who was really frightened was my Toppi! And yet he alone could *know* that all my words were lies! It was so unbearably ridiculous when I met his pleading frightened eyes, that I abruptly ended my speech, suddenly, at its very climax. Silently, I waved my torn sleeve, which served me as a standard, once or twice, and hurled it into the corner. For a moment it seemed to me that the shaven monkey, too, was frightened: the blue of his cheeks seemed to stand out sharply upon the pale, square face and the little coals of his eyes were glowing suspiciously beneath his black, bushy eyebrows. But he slowly raised his hand and the same sacrilegiously-jesting voice broke the general silence:

"Vade Petro Satanas!"

Or did the Cardinal try to hide behind this jest his actual fright? I do not know. I know nothing. If I could not destroy them, like Sodom and Gomorrah, is it worth while speaking of cold shivers and goose flesh? A mere glass of wine can conquer them.

And Magnus, like the skilled healer of souls that he was, said calmly:

"Will you have a glass of wine, Your Eminence?"

"With pleasure," replied the Cardinal.

"But none for Satan," added Magnus jestingly, pouring out the wine. But he could speak and do anything he pleased now: Wondergood was squeezed dry and hung like a rag upon the arm of the chair.

After the wine had been drunk, Magnus lit a cigarette (he smokes cigarettes), cast his eye over the audience, like a lecturer before a lecture, motioned pleasantly to Toppi, now grown quite pale, and said the following…although he was obviously drunk and his eyes were bloodshot, his voice was firm and his speech flowed with measured calm:

"I must say, Wondergood, that I listened to you very attentively and your passionate tirade created upon me, I may say, a great, artistic impression…at certain points you reminded me of the best passages of Brother Geronimo Savanarola. Don't you also find the same striking resemblance, Your Eminence? But alas! You are slightly behind the times. Those threats of hell and eternal torture with which you might have driven the beautiful and merry Florence to panic ring extremely unconvincing in the atmosphere of contemporary Rome. The sinners have long since departed from the earth, Mr. Wondergood. Have not you noticed that? And as for criminals, and, as you have expressed it, scoundrels,—a plain commissary of police is much more alarming to them than Beelzebub himself with his whole staff of devils. I must also confess that your reference to the court of history and posterity was rather strange when contrasted with the picture you painted of the tortures of hell and your reference to eternity. But here, too, you failed to rise to the height of contemporary thought: every fool nowadays knows that history records with equal impartiality both the names of saints and of rogues. The whole point, Mr. Wondergood, which you, as an American, should be particularly familiar with, is in the scope with which history treats its respective subjects and heroes. The lashings history administers to its great criminals differ but little from her laurels—when viewed at a distance and this little distinction eventually becomes quite invisible—I assure you, Wondergood. In fact, it disappears entirely! And in so far as the biped strives to find a place in history—and we are all animated by this desire, Mr. Wondergood—it need not be particular through which door it enters: I beg the indulgence of His Eminence, but no prostitute received a new guest with greater welcome than does history a new…hero. I fear, Wondergood, that your references to hell as well as those to history have fallen flat. Ah, I fear your hope in the police will prove equally ill-founded: I have failed to tell you that His Eminence has received a certain share of those billions which you have transferred to me in such a perfectly legal manner, while his connections…you understand?"

Poor Toppi: all he could do was to keep on blinking! The *aides* broke into loud laughter, but the Cardinal mumbled angrily, casting upon me the burning little coals of his eyes:

"He is indeed a brazen fellow. He said he is Satan. Throw him out, Signor Magnus. This is sacrilege!"

"Is that so?" smiled Magnus politely: "I did not know that Satan, too, belonged to the heavenly chair…."

"Satan is a fallen angel," said the Cardinal in an instructive tone.

"And as such he is in your service? I understand," Magnus bowed his head politely in acceptance of this truth and turned smilingly to me: "Do you hear, Wondergood? His Eminence is irritated by your audacity."

I was silent. Magnus winked at me slyly and continued with an air of artificial importance:

"I believe, Your Eminence, that there must be some sort of misunderstanding here. I know the modesty and well-informed mind of Mr. Wondergood and I suppose that he utilized the name of Satan merely as an artistic gesture. Does Satan ever threaten people with the police? But my unfortunate friend did. And, in general, has anybody ever seen *such* a Satan?"

He stretched his hand out to me in an effective gesture—and the reply to this was another outburst of laughter. The Cardinal, too, laughed, and Toppi alone shook his wise head, as if to say:

"Idiots!"...

I think Magnus must have noticed that. Or else he fell into intoxication. Or was it because that spirit of murder with which his soul was aflame could not remain passive and was tearing at the leash. He threateningly shook his heavy, explosive head and shouted:

"Enough of this laughter! It is silly. Why are you so sure of yourselves? It is stupid, I tell you. I believe in nothing and that is why I admit *everything*. Press my hand, Wondergood: they are all fools and I am quite ready to admit that you are Satan. Only you have fallen into a bad mess, friend Satan. Because it will not save you. I will soon throw you out anyhow! Do you hear...devil?"

He shook his finger at me threateningly and then lapsed into thought, dropping his head low and heavily, with his red eyes ablaze, like those of a bull, ready to hurl himself upon his enemy. The *aides* and the insulted Cardinal were silent with confusion. Magnus again shook his finger at me significantly and said:

"If you are Satan, then you've come here too late. Do you understand? What did you come here for, anyway? To play, you say? To tempt? To laugh at us human beings? To invent some sort of a new, evil game? To make us dance to your tune? Well,—you're too late. You should have come earlier, for the earth is grown now and no longer needs your talents. I speak not of myself, who deceived you so easily and took away your money: I, Thomas Ergo. I speak not of Maria. But look at these modest little friends of mine: where in your hell will you find such charming, fearless devils, ready for any task? And yet they are so small,—they will not even find a place in history."

It was after this that Thomas Magnus blew me up, in the holy city of Rome, in the Palazzo Orsini, when I still belonged to the American billionaire, Henry Wondergood. Do you remember that genial American with his cigar and patent gold teeth? Alas! He is no longer with us. He died suddenly and you will do well if you order a requiem mass for him: his Illinois soul is in need of your prayers.

Let us receive the last breath of Henry Wondergood, blown up by the culprit Thomas Magnus, and buried by Maria in the evening, when the moon was shining brightly.

THE END

***